SEARCHING *for*
ATTICUS

JANICE HARVEY

This is a work of fiction. All characters in this book are the product of the author's imagination. Any businesses, organizations, places, events, and incidents are used fictionally. Any resemblance to a real person, living or dead, is a tremendous coincidence.

Copyright © 2022 by Janice Harvey
All rights reserved

ISBN 978-1-939351-52-4

Printed in United States of America

Dedication

To the memory of my brother Kevin,
my first teacher.

And to Sheryll O'Brien,
who taught me to trust my words.

"She was powerful, not because she wasn't scared but because she went on so strongly despite the fear."

                        Harper Lee

History in the Making

Until those shots were fired, it had been a regular old Friday at Hammond Street Elementary. When it was time for dismissal, I couldn't find my hat.

The coatroom outside Miss McDonald's class was swarming with kids, everybody shoving, fidgety with anticipation. When I found it, I pulled the hand-knitted cap over my head without tying it under my chin. I let the strings dangle, tickling my neck as I slipped my arms into the coat that used to be my cousin's.

Miss McDonald wasn't "liking this noise, children," and she said so only once. Everybody settled down, knowing we wouldn't be allowed to form our patrol line if we were making any noise. We were quiet as church mice then, because her arms were folded, and we all knew what that meant.

When we finally got outside, the air hit my legs hard. (We girls still had to wear dresses all the time back then, with the exception of snow pants under our skirts on snow days, and my legs were bare, but for my white ankle socks. My mother didn't believe a fourth-grader was old enough for knee socks, and I'd have to be 13 before I'd get my hands on a garter belt and stockings. The fuzzy hair on my shins stood right up against the chill; it would be years before I was deemed an appropriate age for leg-shaving.)

Charles Kendall was patrol line leader, a job he took as seriously as Moses took the tablets. His orange safety belt was draped across last year's plaid wool coat. Sixth grade had made a man out of Charles Kendall, alright. And a bully of a man, I noticed.

My partner was Deborah Rice. We held hands, and tried not to talk until we were around the corner at St. Bernadette's Church, but with Charles barking out orders like a grown-up, Deborah couldn't keep quiet.

"I'm not impressed a bit. He's such a dick," she breathed into my ear, and I felt my face grow crimson from the word that I knew meant "penis," another word I couldn't actually say out loud. I wondered how Richard Dumphy could stand his name, especially when his mother yelled "Dicky, you get in here now!" at the top of her lungs from the third-floor porch of the Dirty Block.

We walked up Hammond Street to Chestnut, and Deborah let her palm slap against St. Bernadette's iron fence. At the corner, Charles Kendall held his hand up like a traffic cop, but something caught his eye. Instead of bullying us back into formation, he squatted down over two bundles of The Evening Gazette, our late-afternoon newspaper. Kids were falling out of line everywhere, and Charles Kendall wasn't even yelling at them.

Deborah yanked my hand hard, pulling me up to where our patrol line leader crouched. When we were close enough, I heard Deborah say "Holy shit," and she pushed me to look over Charles Kendall's shoulder.

In all my nine years, I'd never seen headlines so big and black. They floated above two pictures, capital letters in the blackest ink. I didn't need to get any closer to see them; there were only two words:

PRESIDENT DEAD

"Gimme that belt, Kendall. If you aren't plannin' on crossin' then I'll do it," sixth-grader Edward Kline shouted. "Principal Gleason will kick your sorry ass if one of them kindergarten brats gets squished under a city bus."

Charles Kendall slipped off the belt and handed it to Edward without a word. He looked like he'd been hypnotized. Deborah yanked me once more, and we walked the rest of the way home without words. There was nothing to say about something so strange happening on an ordinary day.

"I'm home, Twig," I said, as I pushed open the kitchen door. I could smell potato pancakes frying in my mother's electric skillet. No meat, I remembered, not on Friday.

I came around the corner to the pantry slowly. Twig looked up from the splattering grease with a squint. She'd been crying, still was. An L&M cigarette was attached to her bottom lip; like magic, it stuck to her skin and moved when she spoke.

"The president's dead," we both said, followed by, "Owe me a Coke."

Twig grated a large onion into the bowl of potato batter. I could see that she'd started these pancakes earlier, because the grated potatoes were darkening up from the air. In a short while, the bowl would be filled with black batter.

The pancakes in the skillet sizzled, growing lacy brown edges. Twig flipped one over, sending its pinkish-gray belly down into the spitting oil.

"A horrible, horrible thing," my mother said between sniffles, "but they got the guy."

Till then, I had no notion the president was actually murdered. I couldn't read the small words over Charles Kendall's shoulder.

"People are so envious of beauty and youth, they just itch to destroy it," Twig boo-hooed.

I followed her into the living room, where she'd been ironing my father's shirts for work. The TV was humming the news of the assassination, grainy images of a hospital in Texas. Walter Cronkite looked very tired; the kind of tired sleep won't cure.

"Killed in cold blood, before his wife and the whole world," Twig cried. Walter Cronkite took his glasses off, put them back on again.

"Where's *The Edge of Night*?" I asked. Twig never missed an episode of her favorite soap opera. Personally, I preferred *Love of Life*.

"My Lord, Molly, our president is dead. Somehow, the goings-on in Monticello seem insignificant," Twig lectured, her cigarette moving a mile a minute. I shrugged.

Mrs. Jacqueline Kennedy appeared on the television screen.

"What's all over her legs, Twig?" I asked.

"That would be the blood and brains of her husband."

Walter Cronkite looked beaten down. So did Twig.

"Our beloved president is dead! His beautiful children are fatherless," she wailed. Even so, I couldn't keep my eyes off Mrs. Kennedy's shins.

———◇———

The center of our universe was that black-and-white television, where perfect families solved problems within the space of 30 minutes, not counting pitches for Winston cigarettes and Nestle's Quik. Size 8 mothers wore dresses and nylon stockings, and vacuumed all day, every day. Wise and wonderful dads sat in arm chairs, spouting platitudes, and dispensing solid advice. But every now and then, I'd look around our apartment during the commercial breaks and wonder where we went so dreadfully wrong.

"You can pick your seat at the movies," my mother would say, "but you can't pick your relatives."

She was baptized Vernice, though I rarely heard her called by that name. She'd been "Twig" since her teasing, mean-spirited father nicknamed her. Battling fat was a life-long occupation for Twig. Her children had not inherited her weight problems; she couldn't decide if she was pleased or disgusted by this twist.

"Genetics," she'd lament, "is nothing more than a god-damned roll of the dice."

Now and then, she'd become unhinged over the futility of dieting, and take steps to curb her desires. A year before, while I was recovering from a vicious case of poison ivy, she bought the safe.

"Bring it in here, doll," I heard her purr to the delivery man. He shoved a dolly over the threshold, stopping for a minute to adjust the straps holding the large steel safe she'd purchased the day before.

Twig ordered the man to place the big box in the far corner of the living room. After signing the papers attached to his clipboard, Twig dismissed him with a wave. She handed me a sealed envelope.

"Molly," she said, "this is the combination to the safe."

"Why are you giving it to me, Twig?" I asked, scratching behind my knee where watery blisters were forming.

"Just open it," she urged.

I obliged, though I wasn't at all sure why. When the door swung open, Twig headed into the kitchen. After a few minutes, she returned with full arms.

I watched as Twig carefully stacked a box of Oreos, two cartons of Ring-Dings, a sleeve of Girl Scout Thin Mints and one half-dozen Oh!Henry bars inside the safe. She took one last look at the stash before closing the door. Twig spun the dial with great fanfare, as if she were launching an ocean liner.

"Done!" she declared.

"What's this all about, Vernice?" I asked.

"Don't call me that," she warned.

The safe, she explained, would be her salvation.

"Molly, I won't wear men's shorts to the beach again this year. I just won't," she said, patting the safe like a golden retriever. If it had a chin, she would've scratched under it. If all the goodies in the house were locked inside, Twig reasoned, she'd have no choice but to eat healthy snacks.

"Like apples. Oranges. Stuff like that," she told me. She glanced around the apartment. "Do we have any of that around here?"

I didn't know. I was too busy fretting over the idea of keeping those Girl Scout Thin Mints out of reach.

"What about Arlene and me, Twig? Can't we ever eat another sweet thing?" I worried.

"You have the combination, Molly. Just don't open it for me, no matter how much I beg. Hear me?"

This seemed absurd, but I knew Twig was serious. She'd tried on a bathing suit earlier in the week. I heard her howling way out back, by the cyclone fence, where I was tugging on vines I would soon discover were poison ivy. I'd seen the tank suit fly out the kitchen window like some flag of surrender, floating to the ground below.

Now, a year later, the murder of our president had proved too much for Twig. This calamity sent her to the safe. She saw Kennedy as part of our extended family, one of her own. November 22 would bear a big black X on every calendar that hung in our kitchen, for the rest of Twig's life.

"Now, open the safe," she said to me.

"No way," I answered.

"Come on. Open the safe." she repeated.

"You said never, not even if you begged," I told her.

"Please? I'll make fudge if you do."

"No way, Vernice, nuh-uh."

"Don't call me that," she warned.

Twig was never what the doctors call obese. She was muscular, and wide, a big woman with a grand pile of chestnut brown hair that teetered precariously like a listing ship. She was stronger than she was heavy, like a wrestler, but no amount of telling her such a thing would make a dent in her self-image.

"When you mean FAT, say it. There's no sense dressing it up for a party it's not likely to attend," she'd say.

It didn't help that my father was of slight build. Nearly five inches shorter and thirty pounds lighter, Frank was bird-like, with slim hips and narrow wrists that Twig could've snapped like pussy willow branches.

"The man has no ass to speak of," she'd marvel.

Frank sold soda for Canada Dry, which didn't help Twig keep the weight off. She suckled a bottle of grape "tonic," as we called it up here in New England, from morning till night. The empty glass bottles were stored in their wooden cases, stacked higher than Twig's hair-do, in the barn out back.

Those bottles would've netted me a nickel a piece, if Frank didn't return them for redemption himself. What we didn't know was that little bird-like Frank saved every nickel that came from the bottles emptied by Twig. By fall of that same year, Frank had enough spare change to take a trip to see the Alamo. He left on a raw November day in 1963, only two days before Lee Harvey Oswald shot President John F. Kennedy dead in the very same state of Texas, sending Twig to the safe, sobbing nearly non-stop for close to a week.

We checked the mail regularly but received only one measly postcard from Frank, telling us how we shouldn't judge all of Texas by the behavior of one wingnut. He said it was fine country, wide open and warm, with a horizon unlike any we'd ever seen back here in the city of seven hills. And that postcard was the last we heard from Frank.

Suddenly, I had a lot more in common with that prissy Caroline Kennedy than just the state of Massachusetts.

Weighing the Odds

We've lived all our lives in the smack dead center of Massachusetts, in a place that measures like a city and thinks like a town. Standing in front of City Hall, the word "metropolis" would never cross your lips, though we are, by definition, the second-largest city in the state.

The central Mass. accent includes no "R." Mother is **muthah** and father is **fahthah** and you might need a **quatah** for the cigarette machine. Frank used to say if you lived here, your alphabet had only 25 letters. Maybe he chose Texas as a refuge because it has no "R."

None of this should be confused with the Boston accent, which is quite different from ours, or the Kennedy accent which is an accent all its own. The Kennedys were apparently so wealthy they were able to purchase their own sound. Nobody sounds like a Kennedy - nobody on the North Shore, the South Shore, Newbury Street, Beacon Hill or Cape Cod. When you watch any movie with characters from Boston, you'll hear the lamest attempts at Kennedy-esque speechifying imaginable. I've yet to hear a Boston accent replicated accurately, unless the actors were born in Dawchestah.

That said, during the spring of 1964, Lyndon Johnson was our president, the Beatles were God, and Cassius Clay knocked Sonny Liston on his ass. Downtown was still the heart of the city where we lived. Main Street still bustled back then. Nowadays, you can walk a two-mile stretch and rarely bump into another soul, but it was a healthy, vibrant business district, once upon a time.

That was before the biggest white elephant in our city's history swallowed up small businesses like peanuts from a paper sack. Whoever thought it would make sense to drop a gargantuan shopping mall behind City Hall probably invested in the Edsel. Main Street's foot traffic dried up like unwrapped cheese.

But when I was a kid, downtown was a swell place to visit, with storefronts that beckoned, and a policeman directing traffic to ease the snarl. Department stores with names like Barnard's and Filene's and Denholm's drew steady streams of customers, and a trip downtown meant dressing up.

I wore white gloves when I rode Denholm's escalator.

I loved to shop, while Twig hated it thoroughly. She said there was no joy in trying to "wrap the package," and let me know how lucky I was to be able to wear stylish clothes, not that I owned any. Baby sister Arlene and I were built like the Medavoys, Twig said, and out of flimsy material at that.

With Frank's "extended tour of the Southwest," as Twig described it to outsiders, my mother decided to reevaluate the circumstances of her life. This involved a lot of staring into the long mirror nailed to the back of her bedroom door.

She was 38 years old and built like a linebacker, she said, "not exactly in demand."

So Twig set out to be "in demand," and her first step toward achieving seductress status began with the ceremonial smashing of her last case of grape tonic. It galled her to think she'd provided Frank with the ticket out of his life with us.

"This crap'll never fill the Frigidaire again," she announced, tossing 24 bottles of purple bubbly into the trash cans from our second-floor porch. Her aim was flawless, never once missing her target. When the last bottle crashed into the tin, she let out a dramatic sigh.

"I should've snapped him in half on our honeymoon," she said.

Dieting followed this ceremony. I lost track of how many different types of diets she tried. I do recall the tiny scale she used to weigh her food, for a while. For two weeks, Twig wouldn't eat a thing unless it was first placed on the scale.

I came home from school one afternoon just in time to see the scale fly from the open kitchen window, much like the bathing suit had the year before. Only the scale didn't land as gently.

"You almost killed Arlene," I shouted, standing below the window. My three-year-old sister squatted happily in the brown patch of grass that was our yard, playing with the twisted scale that could have been her instrument of death. Arlene was forever harnessed to the clothesline pole, and blissfully refusing to join the toilet-trained. She smiled at nothing with teeth the size of Chiclets, her beautiful head of thick red curls filled with dirt and grass clippings. It was not Arlene's way to look anyone in the eye, and she was uninterested in most normal play. Her idea of a fun time was lining up rocks on the sidewalk. We call it autism nowadays, but in 1964, there was no common name for what was wrong with Arlene, though "retahded" was on the lips of most neighbors.

In truth, I was weary of Twig's problems. Arlene couldn't understand, and didn't care. It fell on me, as the oldest, to act as the sounding board for my mother, and Twig unloaded her miseries on me daily.

"I married your father late in life, Molly. 25 was *old* for a girl to be marrying, unless she was a war widow on her second go-round. I really thought I'd be an old maid, Like Aunt Blanche. I spent what is called my "formative years" with that old woman, going to the movies, smoking cigarettes. It was Aunty who taught me how to blow smoke from my nose," blah-blahhed Twig.

I was quickly tiring of the never-ending story of Vernice. Twig as narrator meant holes in the story, great cavities through which the truth might slip unnoticed. I had better things to do than sit in our smoke-filled kitchen and listen to chapter 100 of the woes of Twig. I had plans.

On Saturday, I'd go out right after breakfast and not return until lunch. Behind the dilapidated garage, I'd stashed a big rectangle of corrugated cardboard. The two fat Gagne sisters tossed it out after their new refrigerator arrived, and I snatched it up quick. It was my plan to use the flattened box as a magic carpet, riding it down the already-green hill behind the garage.

Come Saturday, it was still dark out when I climbed from bed. Even though I was afraid of darkness most of the time, I loved this morning kind of dark. It felt different from the darkness that froze me up so I couldn't move.

I was good at being quiet when I needed to be. I tip-toed into the parlor and clicked on the TV, but first I turned the volume knob way down low. That early, most channels had test patterns that delivered a horrible squeal, and I wasn't ready to share my Saturday morning with Twig just yet. Arlene could sleep through the Battle of Little Big Horn, but Twig was another story.

I twisted the dial until I found George Burns and his foolish wife Gracie. I just loved the old shows, especially the way Mr. Burns talked into the screen, to the people watching at home. It made me feel like I was somebody he trusted.

George Burns was never on television after dawn, so if I wanted to watch him puff his cigar and try to understand his wife, I had to be an early bird. When I had the volume adjusted just-so, I curled up on the sofa with my best doll, Chatty Cathy. I'd gotten her last Christmas, but I had to hide her on the shelf in the long closet so that Arlene wouldn't bust her string and leave her speechless. Not that anything Cathy said made sense. That's why I almost never used her that way; I made up her words myself.

I was getting hungry, but I wouldn't open the fridge. I knew Twig would lumber out by 6:30, and I could wait. I didn't go in for a pee, either, because the toilet paper holder was loud, and the flush was like a volcanic eruption.

I was watching the man selling pans with the pistol-grip handles, when the door to what used to be my parents' bedroom opened. Twig came out, quiet as me. She brushed my too-short bangs back when she walked by, and it felt good, her hand on my head like that.

I could smell coffee perking soon enough, and it was my favorite morning smell. Frank always said Twig's coffee tasted like mud, but I loved it. She let me pour my own, and add two big spoonfuls of sugar with the milk.

In the kitchen, my mother had her first cigarette of the day burning in the ashtray. The smoke curled up around her puffy face, but her eyes didn't squint up the way mine did.

"Go out to the stoop for the paper, Molly," Twig told me, and I was light on my big feet as I stepped out to retrieve The Morning Telegram from our second-floor porch. Our paperboy was good old almost-a-man Charles Kendall.

I snatched up the second half of the paper while Twig went for the obituaries and the arrests. I needed to know if Brenda Starr would find her true love, Basil St. John; I had to see what she was wearing on a Saturday morning. Of course, it wasn't like Sunday, when the newspaper was heavy and landed with a thud on the stoop. That paper was wrapped in color funnies.

This morning, Brenda was not lolling around almost bare-naked in a cave with a black orchid stuck behind her ear, so I moved on to Gasoline Alley. I'd have to wait for The Evening Gazette to check on the girls from Apartment 3-G.

That's when I remembered two things about Saturday. One was wonderful, and the other wasn't at all. After breakfast, I could watch cartoons. That was the wonderful. Confession was the not-at-all-wonderful part of Saturday.

Twig put breakfast on the table in a short while, hot Cream of Wheat cereal and challah bread sliced thick and toasted in the broiler. I poured a second cup of coffee and sat down to this feast, surprised by my growling stomach. I drizzled just a little milk over the cereal, and dropped a dollop of butter and a spoonful of sugar in the center of the mound. Twig came in from the pantry and sprinkled my cereal with a dusting of cinnamon. I looked up at her with a smile, but she'd already turned away, and didn't catch my happiness.

I took my One-A-Day vitamin. I had to rush through breakfast if I was going to see Rex Trailer on channel 4. His show was on for hours, but early in the morning, it began in his bunkhouse. Rex rode Gold Rush, his beautiful horse, over hills and prairies to get there, singing:

Hoofbeats, hoofbeats, hoofbeats
Thunder 'cross the prairie wide

Hoofbeats, hoofbeats, hoofbeats
Ride, Cowboy, ride!

Rex had a friend named Pablo, a Mexican. Pablo didn't get to ride a spiffy horse like Rex. Pablo had a worn-out donkey that appeared to be one trot away from the glue factory, with a woolen blanket tossed over its back, instead of a swell saddle like the one Rex put on Gold Rush. And Pablo acted kind of stupid most of the time, especially after the donkey kicked him in the head. He was gone for a few weeks after that happened, and when he came back to the bunkhouse, he was wearing a bandage.

I wondered if Frank ever ran into Rex, out there in Texas. Sometimes, I imagined my father thundering 'cross the prairie wide. Little bird-like Frank, perched atop a stallion taller than Twig, somehow riding despite the handicap of having no ass to speak of.

Frank not being with us simply made for a different sort of quiet; the empty kind we couldn't fill with noise. Before my father's departure, he'd sit at the breakfast table with Twig, though two words never passed between them. They'd sit with their morning faces buried behind pages of the newspaper. They didn't even say "Good morning" to each other. And though I was accustomed to their chill, I knew it wasn't like that in other houses.

When I slept at Kathleen Higgins' house, I noticed her parents saying plenty to each other in the morning, words like: "How'd you sleep?" "Would you like some eggs?" and "Come read the paper while I get that for you."

And they kissed. Not like in the movies, but real easy, like they didn't even know they were doing it, because they were so used to kissing in the morning. No one was leaving for work or anything like that. Imagine that: They just kissed for the kissing of it.

Twig was reading Dear Abby. I could see her if I tilted my head back far enough. Her second cigarette was one long ash. I wanted another mug of that coffee, but I knew the answer would be "No." Not for any real reason, but because Twig sometimes liked to exercise her option to use the word.

Arlene climbed from her crib and padded across the parlor floor, rubbing her eye hard with the heel of her palm. I didn't say her name, because she smelled like pee, and I didn't want her crawling all over me. If she spotted Chatty Cathy, she'd toss a tantrum till I let her pull the string. I wasn't about to let smelly old Arlene silence my best Christmas present.

On the screen, Rex gave way to cartoons. I watched Popeye squeeze spinach from a can. Soon enough, Bluto was getting his bum beat by the rejuvenated sailor, which pleased me. I snapped off the TV, put Chatty Cathy back on the shelf and got myself dressed for play, in Saturday clothes. I chose corduroys with the knees going white from wear, and tennis shoes with holes where the big toes should be. Pushing the thought of Confession out of my head, I concentrated instead on the magnificent piece of abandoned cardboard waiting for me.

In March, the gray month, we had more snow on the TV screen than on the ground. Outside, Deborah and I played hop-scotch right through the winter, something I couldn't remember ever doing before. Spring thaw arrived with nothing to melt.

We played outside because there was nothing to do inside, but outside was dull, too. We formed a club, but we were the only members, so not much happened at our meetings. We plotted the torture of girls we thought pretty, but mostly we spent our time re-pinning the old blanket we used for a roof. On a Saturday morning, Deborah would not be awake yet - she loved to sleep, while the joys of lolling in bed thoroughly escaped me.

"Jack Ruby is going to die for his patriotism," Twig muttered into her coffee cup, not looking up from her newspaper.

"A jury found him guilty of killing the man who shot President Kennedy, that horrible Lee Harvey Oswald."

I'd watched that murder with eyes opened big as dinner plates. Mr. Ruby shot Mr. Lee Harvey Oswald on television, bold as brass. He just walked right up and jammed a gun into the man's belly, killing him as easy as going up to Mae at Elmer & Bill's corner store and saying: "I'd like a Planter's Peanut Bar, please."

I watched Ruby shoot Oswald over and over again, courtesy of the magic of video tape, and I still couldn't figure out why he died. The gun looked so small, and it wasn't as if his head got blown to bits like the president. Why couldn't a man take a teeny bullet in the belly and live?

When Jack Ruby killed Oswald within days of the president's murder, Twig said Ruby was "a bona fide hero, shooting that evil Communist bastard Oswald." My grandmother had different ideas about the man who killed Kennedy's assassin. Her eyebrow flew up when she heard the words "nightclub owner."

"Doesn't sound like a patriot to me," was all she said. Twig held fast to her admiration of Ruby. I knew better than to question her about it, even now, with Ruby going to prison, and maybe even the gallows. I had stuff to do, and outside, spring had finally arrived.

Seeing Things

  Once I was out on the stoop, I took the deepest breath I could take. I wore last year's spring jacket for play, and my arms were too long for it. My wrists stuck out of the sleeves all pale and thin like Frank's arms, two hairy, freckled birch branches. I let out my breath nice and slow; it felt good just to be out and away from Twig's L&Ms.

  The cardboard was still where I hid it, and it was as big as I remembered. Two people could sit on it, if Deborah Rice came to play later, I'd consider letting her slide with me. I might even cut it in two, I thought, if her mood was nice enough. Sometimes, she was a tad hateful, but I knew why. If the Rice family had a volume knob, it would be stuck on HIGH permanently. Her dad worked for the sanitation department, an Irishman, and her mother was "100% Italian," and she'd tell you so, especially within earshot of Mr. Rice, as if this information had previously been withheld from the man she married. This made for some craziness in their kitchen. Once, I went home in the middle of the night instead of staying over, because I just couldn't listen to the brawling. It didn't seem to bother Deborah, but it frightened me. The angry words of other families are harder to hear than your own people squabbling.

I rode the cardboard two or three times, until I grew tired of playing alone. The hill seemed shorter with each ride. After a while, I sat at the peak and tore small pieces from the Frigidaire box, allowing the wind to pick them up and carry them over the fence to the Dirty Block, where they would go unnoticed forever.

From where I sat, I could peer under the garage. Built on the same slant of land that created my little hill, the garage was propped up by concrete pillars on the side where it jutted out over sloping grass. This made a crawlspace, and every kid in our neighborhood knew about it. At its roomiest point, near the pillars, the crawlspace wasn't much taller than me. Even *I* had to stoop most of the time. Bigger kids hogged the far end to keep from getting stiff necks, or having to sit on the ground with younger kids.

The ground beneath it was all dirt, rocks, and chunks of broken glass. Long ago the older neighborhood boys had dragged slab rocks from the

Dirty Block wall that supported the Dirty Block fence, and made seats for themselves. Leaving my not-so-magic carpet behind, I went there, claiming a rock for a chair, something I'd never have a chance to do if big kids happened by.

I used the torn toe of my Saturday tennis shoe to kick at the ashes left by a small fire started with stolen matches. A crumpled magazine page caught my eye, and when I smoothed it out on my knee, I was looking at something I shouldn't be seeing: a mostly naked woman. Her bare breasts were VERY big, with pointy brown nipples. Her privates were visible, because she was sitting just the way Twig said not to: with wide-open legs.

A furry red hat and black patent-leather boots were all she'd managed to wriggle into before the photographer snapped her picture. I took a long look at this; I was fairly certain that my body would never erupt into any shape coming close to Santa's Helper. Her smiling face made a quivery feeling rise inside of me, a feeling like nothing I knew. I wasn't at all sure about this business of being bare-naked for all the world to see. I wasn't sure about anything that had to do with bodies. In fact, I'd already had a big fight with Martha Farrell over this very subject.

I invited her to play Barbies at my house after school one Wednesday. I got my first Barbie for my 10th birthday, in January; not the one I wanted with the silky red ponytail, but the one with the brown bubble-cut. Martha had a vinyl Barbie *carry-case*, with **Barbie** printed on it. It was fuchsia-colored, and filled with outfits hanging on tiny pink hangers. I kept my Barbie in a Keds shoebox. I didn't have the good Barbie clothes, the ball gowns and the bathing suits. My not-really-an-aunt Annie made most of my Barbie's outfits, and I hated taking them out in front of Martha. None of these dresses said "Mattel" inside.

We were pretending that Martha's Barbie was adopted and searching for her real parents when Martha told me that she had amazing information to share with me. She said she couldn't say it out loud where anyone might hear, so we crawled under my bed.

"I know how babies get here," she said. This was a valuable piece of the big puzzle of life. I needed to hear it.

"The man puts his thing inside the woman's thing. That's how babies grow."

I was stunned. And angry. I whispered my maddest "My mother would never do that!" and I told her to take her fancy Barbie crap home.

I was so busy marveling over the improbability of ever looking like Santa's Helper that I didn't hear Bernard Ducharme and William Sparhawk until they scrunched down right in front of me.

"Off the rocks, Pisspot," Bernard told me, and I obeyed, stuffing the crumpled porn into my jeans pocket. My face grew warm with guilt as I found a place to squat. We were in a place where kids went to do things they shouldn't.

Bernard was in the sixth grade, all bones and skin and little else. Under the garage, bent in half, he needed to sit. His neck hurt too much to stand, all folded up like a Japanese fan.

The older boys didn't mind me much because I wasn't a squealer and I made them laugh, walking like Mr. Gleason, or impersonating old Miss Davis with her shrill voice and her turkey neck. But they didn't look at me the way they looked at Deborah, and that bothered me sometimes.

William Sparhawk stood just a little bit bent beneath the garage. He was black-haired and black-eyed like his older sister Naomi, a high school cheerleader whose looks were like none other. William Sparhawk was every bit as beautiful as Naomi, and I couldn't keep my eyes off him.

Bernard pulled a pint bottle of something called Peppermint Schnapps from his back pocket, stolen from his father's overcoat. I said: "No, thank you," when he offered it my way, but William took a mouthful. He tried not to make a terrible face when he swallowed, but I could see that it made him want to spit.

That was when he turned around so that I could see him sideways. He unzipped his pants and started peeing against the cement wall. His urine washed all over and down in streams, and I knew I should look away, but I didn't. He looked over at me and smiled, and tucked the pink head back inside his Levis.

"Whattaya lookin' at, Molly?" Bernard asked me, laughing. When he stood up he was unsteady on his feet.

"She's lookin' at my pecker, aren't you, Molly? Maybe you'd like it if I took it out again?" William moved his fingers toward his zipper.

I was on my feet pretty quick then, and I could hear them whooping it up under the garage all the way to my house. I was breathing like I might die by the time I reached my back door, when a paralyzing thought came to me.

I'd have to tell Father Vail about this in Confession. I wasn't at all sure if seeing the Sparhawk penis qualified as a sin. And was it my sin or William's? I couldn't figure out if not looking away would book me a room in Hell for eternity. And if it *was* a sin, how could I word it so that I wouldn't commit yet another sin by using the word "penis" in the house of God?

This was worrisome, much more so than actually seeing William Sparhawk's penis. It would be a long, long afternoon, waiting to know.

Dodging Damnation

Twig wasn't going with me to Confession. In fact, she never went anymore. It was her opinion that she'd been sinned *against*, and was deserving of life-long absolution for having to endure the humiliation and suffering of being abandoned by a man with no ass to speak of.

My green plaid dress with the white collar was ironed and ready by 3:30. I dragged my feet around all day, hoping I could make her believe I was dying of polio. I put my forehead against the oven door when she wasn't looking, trying to create the illusion of fever.

"Nice try," she said as I pulled the plaid smocking over my head.

"Listen, Vernice, I don't see the point of this confession stuff," I complained.

"Don't call me that," she warned. "You know you have to go, Molly. We have this same conversation every Saturday. If you want to sleep at Nana's house tonight, you'd better stop belly-aching now. I've got a lot on my mind and I don't need to hear you whine about holy obligations to God."

Nana's – I'd just about forgotten about spending the night with my grandmother. I had to go through with this horrible task now.

Twig dug bobby pins into my scalp, securing the lace *mantilla* to my head.

"I don't see why I have to wear this silly beanie. Why can't I go bare-headed like the boys do? What sin will I commit if I'm bare-headed, will you tell me please, Twig?" I fidgeted and winced while she scraped my skull.

"The sin of disrespect, Miss Smartypants."

The church wasn't filled with sinners just yet. I blessed myself with Holy Water, and slipped into the third pew from the back, on Father Vail's side. I knew never to go to Father DiStefano. He was younger, and apt to listen carefully to your sins. Twig once told me:

"Always go to Vail because he doesn't give a shit if you robbed a bank, stabbed your mother, blew through the money and buried the body. He's too old and deaf to care." It was just like Twig to force me to go, yet slip me valuable tips on how to work around it.

Father Vail was a "one Our Father, two Hail Marys" kind of priest. No matter what your sin was, he had the standard punishment waiting. Kicking my cousin Daphne under the Thanksgiving dinner table and fibbing got me the same sentence. I wasn't sure if anything involving a penis might warrant a stiffer penalty, so to speak, like maybe an "Act of Contrition." Maybe even three or four of those, the "Oh my God I am heartily sorry for having offended Thee"s.

Offended was the key word here. Maybe glimpsing a penis was just offensive, instead of criminal. The line of sinners was moving right along, which meant that I'd soon find out if I'd have to say a bunch of prayers or gouge my eyes out with a vegetable peeler.

I sat beside Eugene Hastings' mother. She had rosary beads wound through her knobby fingers, and she was praying a mile a minute. I suspected she was making a pitch for Mr. Hastings' soul. He was known to "step out," according to Twig. I heard her on the phone to Aunt Annie one day:

"That bastard barber Chet Hastings has been stepping out on poor Lou since the beginning of time, and he doesn't even try to hide it," she said.

I wasn't sure what "stepping out" entailed, but it was no good, I knew that much. I'd seen Mr. Hastings step out of his barber shop to sweep hair into the gutter. He most certainly did not try to hide it.

The line of Commandment-breakers waiting to spill their guts moved snake-like, and I slid to the right every few minutes. In the far corner of St. Bernadette's, candles burned.

I tried to catalog two weeks' worth of misdeeds: pilfering three *Squirrel-Nuts* from Elmer & Bill's, yanking Arlene's hair, lying bold-as-brass to a bill collector who was trying to find Twig. Gawking at the Sparhawk penis.

I was deep in worry when Mrs. Hastings came from behind the blood-red velvet curtain of Father Vail's confessional. "Reluctantly" doesn't quite explain how I entered his chamber and knelt inside. I waited for Father Vail to finish condemning and forgiving the sinner on the other side of his little closet. I blessed myself like it was a race when I heard the window slide open, and I could see the outline of the parish priest through the vented partition. His head was down and he rubbed the back of his neck. Even his silhouette looked tired.

"BlessmeFatherforIhavesinned," I began, and right away I was in trouble because I didn't go to Confession last week. I thought quickly and added:

"It's been one week since my last Confession. I accuse myself of lying."

This covered me, I believed.

He didn't lift his head, I could tell. I rolled fast and furious into my list of violations:

"Ipulledmysister'shair.Iliedformymother.ItookacoupleextraSquirrelNutsfromElmer&Bill's.Isawaboy'spenis.AndIreturnedabooktotheBookmobilewiththesignoutcardmissingfromtheback.Andblamedmysister."

There.

"Your penance is to say two Our Fathers and two Hail Marys. Go child, and sin no more," he told me in his most weary voice.

That's it? I thought. Not even an Act of Contrition? His head was still down. He didn't even flinch at the "P" word.

"Amen," I whispered, and I was back on the sidewalk so fast, the Holy Water was still wet on my forehead.

Sweet Meat

Having received absolution for my private viewing, my close brush with eternal damnation didn't stop me from wondering about what I'd seen. I kept trying to reconcile that explosive piece of information from Martha Farrell with what I'd seen under the garage.

Plainly speaking, I couldn't fathom that "A" would fit into "B." How could the bitty equipment William Sparhawk sported match up with Miss December's apparatus? I tried to forget what I'd learned from Martha and needed to know more about. I didn't dare ask Twig. She was all tangled up in a new diet, what with summer coming soon.

She'd somehow gotten it into her head that a diet of nothing but meat would chisel her figure. She suffered this brainstorm while we were sprawled out on the sofa, eating *State Line* potato chips and watching *Wild Kingdom.*

"Would you look at those cheetahs?" she marveled. "I bet there isn't an ounce of fat on those creatures! That's because they eat nothing but meat, Molly."

I looked at her sideways. Twig was no slim cat.

"Maybe the answer has been right there, in the wilds of Africa, all along. Maybe that's the key to losing weight for good." She sat up straight after this thought.

"I'm going to try it," she told me.

"You do that, Vernice," I said.

"Don't call me that," she warned.

I was positively light-hearted during the weeks that followed my confession. Not only had I weaseled my way out of permanent residency in Hell, but I was also spending the night at my Nana's house nearly every Saturday, and leaving home early enough to dodge Confession. Nana never made me go. She said that if she wanted to talk to God about a private matter, she'd just call his name.

"It doesn't require a middle man," she said.

I had my clothes packed in a brown paper bag bright and early, so that I could simply grab my sack and fly after a week of Miss McDonald's torturous attempts at making me right-handed.

How I wished that old cow would get it through her thick head that I wasn't ever going to be anything but a southpaw. Making me hold my pencil "correctly" in my left hand wouldn't work, either. Miss McDonald stood over me with blast-furnace breath. I tried my best to make my hand glide from left to right across the paper, even as she insisted that I keep my palm down flat, like a righty. Any left-handed person knows these two movements are as impossible to perform simultaneously as rubbing your belly and patting your head.

Evidently the real burr in Old McDonald's skivvies was the smudged-ink problem: No lefty can write without dragging a hand clear across the fresh ink.

In order to hold the pen and move from one margin to the other (1/2 inch wide, measured meticulously, and drawn with a No.2 pencil, NEVER pen, Dearie) a lefty must curl the hand up, nearly into a fist, and snake it to the other side. The result is a messy paper and a blue hand, wrist and shirt sleeve.

I tried explaining this to that sourpuss McDonald. Her solution was to whack my knuckles with a wooden ruler every time I lifted my palm from the paper. I wasn't sure what she thought would come from making my hand too sore to write with. No matter that keeping my palm flat meant cramping my whole left arm and bumping my elbow into my left rib cage before I could even get my first name down on the paper. It was as if my whole body stood in the way of penmanship. Clearly the Palmer method of penmanship was not designed for lefties. Her damp snorts on the back of my neck made my shoulders jerk up.

"Mary Katherine Medavoy! Why must you be so stubborn?" She'd plead, but I couldn't please the woman. I couldn't write right-handed any more than I could jump into a swinging jump rope. That's why I always took steady ends.

But staying at my Nana's meant erasing the week's struggles. On Saturday morning, Twig walked me to the freshly-painted-mint-green clapboard house at the corner of Oak and Chestnut. It wasn't very far from our tenement, but it involved crossing Chestnut Street, something Twig seemed to think I never did without her. In truth, I'd been crossing that busy stretch of road for more years than I could recall, but she hadn't caught me. Yet.

Twig and her mother never seemed to have much to say to one another. You could slice the tension with a machete whenever they got together. I couldn't understand it, because when Nana and I were alone, we talked our fool heads off.

"How's it going, Vernice?" Nana asked, and I watched Twig count to 10 before answering.

"Doan call me dat," Arlene piped up from her stroller.

Twig gave a weak, embarrassed smile and said: "Hush."

"Fine, Ma. You?"

"Fine, fine. You find work yet?" Nana asked. This was sure to rankle my mother. Twig's nest egg was just about dried up, and Frank wasn't sending us any cash to live on since he'd abandoned us for the breath-taking vistas of elsewhere.

"Not yet, Ma. Still looking," she mumbled.

Now, that was a lie. Twig wasn't looking at all. She was devoted to losing weight the cheetah way, by consuming pounds of red meat and nothing else, which brings me to one of the many reasons why I wanted to stay at Nana's: Lately, Twig smelled bad.

I noticed it around the second week of her skinny-as-a-cat diet. Twig's breath had suddenly become most foul, like finding a dead mouse too late.

And her other end was pretty rancid, too. It was impossible to enter the bathroom after Twig had visited. She smelled worse than Frank ever did, worse than his powerful combination of White Owl cigars and diner-food diet. Worse than Arlene's most horrific diaper.

"Hey, Vernice, what died in here?" I asked, holding my nose between two fingers.

"Light a match," she answered in an injured voice, adding:

"And don't call me that."

When Twig leaned over to kiss me good-bye, I turned my head just enough to let her catch my cheek.

"You lose some weight, Vernice?" Nana asked.

Twig lit up like Times Square.

"Why, yes, I did! 11 lbs. You noticed?"

"Sure I noticed. Now if you could just do somethin' with that God-awful breath, you might catch yourself a beau," Nana said.

Twig clamped her hand across her mouth.

"Let's go, Arlene," she said from underneath her palm.

"Have a good one," Nana offered cheerfully. I climbed the stairs to Nana's house.

We stood and watched for a few moments as Twig wheeled the stroller back down Chestnut. For quite aways downstreet, we could still see Arlene's chocolate-covered hand waving a Yodel I'd snatched from the safe. Presently, Nana returned to the afternoon's task, shifting rocks from the stone wall that separated her yard from her neighbor's.

"Some little so-and-so chased his pal over this wall last night and took down half of it," she told me.

She was happiest there, among her bachelor's buttons and zinnias, and anyone could see proof of her joy in the way her flowers grew each spring and summer. Her rose bed was something that strangers stopped to admire, gorgeous climbers that wrapped themselves up trellises and walls. In May, a sea of peonies hugged the house, near the bulkhead, and in August, a Rose of Sharon tree blossomed right outside the kitchen window, bursting with pink, inviting hummingbirds to visit and sip.

I knew the names of all of these flowers because she explained everything about gardening when we were outside together.

She taught me how to transplant the elegant iris plants, being careful not to harm the delicate roots when I twisted my shovel down into the soil. She showed me how to snap the dried heads from marigolds and save the seeds for next season.

Nana recycled long before it was called any such thing, long before it was mandated by municipal law. Garbage rarely made it to the curbside. Most of her food scraps went into a compost pile in the corner of her garden. She covered the rotting food with a layer of grass clippings, encouraging the whole mess to ferment.

Eggshells never went into the compost. They floated in a milk bottle filled with water that stank to high heaven. Nana said that this putrid elixir was chock full of vitamins the flowers needed, and she watered her house plants with it, too. Coffee grounds never went to waste; instead, she spooned them out around the base of her rose bushes, where they seeped into the soil and strengthened the climbers.

Once, I told Nana she was like Mr. Wizard to me, and she laughed her deep growl-laugh. Her voice was raspy and raw-sounding from the unfiltered *Lucky Strikes* she smoked. Now and then, she called them *fatimas*, but I didn't know why. I just knew to get her a cigarette when she asked.

Nana didn't live alone, though she'd put my grandfather Ben into a nursing home years ago. His legs stopped working back in 1949 she told me, "just before I could leave the miserable gambling bastard," and when he became too ornery to care for, she put him in the big brick building up on Beechwood Hill. That's when her sister-in-law Blanche moved in.

Nana couldn't quite comprehend all the fuss Twig made over Frank's vanishing act. To her, being rid of an aggravating man seemed a blessing. Why whine about less laundry and a smaller grocery bill?

They didn't like each other much, Blanche and my grandmother, but it was cheaper than trying to run the house on her income alone, Nana said, so she let Blanche have the front bedroom and all her meals for 25 dollars a week. It was an "okay set-up," Nana said, so long as she didn't expect anything like work out of Blanche.

After we repaired the wall, we finished raking wet oak leaves away from it. Nana cursed the leaves, because they fell from a tree in the yard across the street, not her yard. The wind carried them to her wall every autumn, where they'd rot till spring if she didn't clear them out.

"Doll, there isn't a God-damned leaf on the Eurlich lawn by first snowfall. Every last one is right here," she grumbled, jabbing the pile with her rake.

"The Eurlichs don't even own a rake," she whispered loudly.

Soon enough, it was suppertime. On Saturdays, this meal would be eaten late in the afternoon, much earlier than most nights. We stored our tools in the small shed she'd constructed from the remains of a garage the Eurlichs tore down a few years back. We left our mud-caked shoes on the back porch.

My Nana was a ghastly cook, though she loved to man the kitchen. She liked to experiment with recipes, changing them by replacing key ingredients with whatever was handy. We ate some terrible suppers on Saturdays, though Aunt Blanche cleaned her plate every time. This afternoon, Nana was making something out of left-over turkey.

She let me stuff the cold meat into the grinder and watch it crawl out the little holes like worms. When it was all ground up, she seasoned it and added bread crumbs and one egg, the shell from which I added to the milk bottle.

She shaped this mixture into softballs; that's what they looked like to me. She placed them on a cookie sheet and baked them in the oven. We ate them with pickled beets, and they were as God-awful as anything she'd ever concocted.

"The *best*," I declared as we cleared the table.

Aunt Blanche retired to the parlor with the Evening Gazette crossword puzzle while Nana and I washed the supper dishes. Blanche's Sunday clothes were laid out already, so that she'd get dressed for 7:00 AM Mass without needing to iron her navy blue skirt. She knew I'd stay home with Nana, and she didn't like it, though she hadn't called us *half-assed Catholics* lately. Nana often said that "Blanche believes her shit doesn't stink," just because she graduated from high school.

Nana and I headed for her bedroom. This was a magical time for me, because Nana was about to get ready for work. I watched her primp and prepare, evolving from landscaper to lady in a wink. I stretched across her bed on my belly while she settled in at the vanity.

My grandmother worked most nights as a waitress at an up-scale restaurant called *Henri's,* which was only "Henry's with smoke blown up your ass and a carved radish," Nana like to say. She'd been working the nightshift there since before World War II. Before that, she waited tables at a little place called Vito's Kitchen. She said she made her best tips waitressing for something she called "New England meetings."

"They loved me because I knew how to keep my mouth shut," she said.

When I asked what was her biggest tip ever, I waited for her to say "Five dollars," or somesuch. Instead, she thought for a minute, and said: "100 bucks from Raymond Patriarca."

I didn't know who that was at the time, but that seemed like an awful lot of change to leave under a coffee cup.

In front of the mirror, she removed a scarf that was wrapped around her head, her *babushka,* she called it. Under it, there must have been a thousand bobby pins. She pulled these out and dropped them into an opalescent dish she kept on her vanity. She waited to comb out these pin-curls, until her make-up was done. I was thankful to be here instead of home, because Twig would be twisting my own hair into these torturous squiggles for Sunday Mass. Sleeping on those things was like resting your head on a barbed-wire fence.

Nana believed in cold cream for the face, and that's what she used to wash away the garden grime. She smeared it on, then tissued it off, and I could see the dirt clinging to the Noxzema. In the bathroom, she washed away the remnants, and returned pink-cheeked, patting her skin gently with a towel. I watched as she drew on the lips "God didn't see fit to give." She created a perfect bow beneath her nose, and filled it in with a creamy red lipstick that made me think of my box of 64 Crayolas. She smiled a big artificial smile to make her cheeks stand up, and dusted them in circular sweeps with pink rouge. *Apples,* she called them.

"Nana," I began, "Why is it that Aunty Blanche never got married?"

Nana stopped her blush brush mid-sweep and looked into the mirror, past herself and into my eyes.

"Because, Doll, she was as homely as a bag of assholes," she told me.

When she combed out her hair, I could see the unruly white hairs darting out from the cinnamon brown ones, renegades that wouldn't stay put. She clipped on a pair of gaudy-beautiful rhinestone earrings, and turned this way and that to survey her work. I rolled back and forth across her bed, still watching her in the vanity mirror.

"Nana, I asked, "Do the chefs get mad when somebody sends food back to the kitchen? I saw that on TV. A man said: 'TAKE THIS AWAY IT'S OVER-DONE AND DREADFUL,' and I just wondered if that hurts the cook's feelings."

"Doll," she told me, "Don't ever send your food back. If it's over-cooked, chew harder. If it's under-cooked, get up and leave. Don't come back. But don't ever send your food back to the kitchen."

"Why?"

"Because," she said to me, "The chef will do terrible things to your dinner."

"Terrible HOW?" I asked.

"Terrible like the NICEST thing he might do is spit in it or step on it. Other things, too, things I can't even speak of because you are a little girl."

This was enough for me. Her voice said so.

Nana shimmied into her uniform and zipped it up over the girdle she'd pushed herself into. She rolled stockings up her legs one at a time, adjusting the heel and toe patches before she clipped the garters. She pulled her bifocals over her head on a chain, and let them dangle against her breasts. They scraped across the name pin that read: YOUR WAITRESS IS ARLENE.

I got up now, and took from her closet her uniform apron. It was my job to tie it just-so around her waist. Ruffled and red, it was starched stiff. I made a bow that was a little too much loop on one side, but Nana looked into the mirror and said:

"Perfect."

At the back door, she slipped on her white leather waitressing shoes, and I bent down to tie these for her. She was the reason I could tie at all, because she was the only other lefty in the family. She once spent a whole Saturday showing me, after everybody else had given up. That was when I was six. I'd become an excellent shoe-tier since.

Nana wore a three-quarter coat with padded shoulders and deep pockets. She carried a cardigan sweater to drape over her shoulders when "things get slow." She slipped a new pack of Luckys into her patent leather handbag, and took taxi fare from the small coin purse with the Chinese dragon stitched on it. She kissed my face.

"Wake me when you come home," I reminded her, and I knew that she would. I wrapped my arms around her waist, inside her coat, and held her tight as could be. When I let go, she kissed me one more time.

"'Bye, Doll," I heard her say as she headed down the walkway.

In the parlor, Aunty already had the TV set on the channel for *Lawrence Welk*, and there would be no changing it. This was not a bit like *Ed Sullivan*, where I might hear someone singing songs I recognized from the radio. I decided to make up my bed.

At Nana's, I slept in the more formal living room, on the sofa, or the divan, as she called it. It was fairly comfortable, but the big problem was the dining room: It was creepy, and I could see it from where I slept. The heavy drapes made strange shadows from the street lights that blazed just outside the house. I dragged two of the high and heavy mahogany chairs from the dining room into the living room, lining them up along the sofa so that when I opened my eyes, all I'd see was wood.

I made my bed with Nana's rose-colored satin comforter and a big feather pillow, and after my bath, I settled into this nest with a book I'd borrowed from the Bookmobile the day before. Without a story to read, I was sure I'd be bored to death by Aunty Blanche and the Lennon Sisters. I opened the cover slowly, savoring that delicious moment when a book was new to me. Books were everything to me; there was never a time when I wasn't buried deep in the middle of one. Tonight, my hands trembled as I turned the first pages of *To Kill a Mockingbird.*

I chose this book because Miss Cronin, the librarian, told me about a movie made from it, starring Mr. Gregory Peck. She saw it at the Plymouth Theater on Main Street. She said:

"Molly, there is a girl in this movie who looks just like you. Her name is Scout."

Reading the jacket of my library book, I discovered that this Harper Lee who wrote it was a *woman.* I thought that was just grand. I hid little snatches of my own poetry between the pages of the Trixie Belden paperbacks I kept on a shelf in my room at home. Being a writer seemed like a fine way to make a living.

I pulled the comforter under my chin and stepped into Maycomb County with Miss Scout

Finch. Already, I loved her, what with her Christian name being Jean Louise. Like me, the name didn't fit the person carrying it.

Hours later, Aunty turned off the light. By then, I'd grown familiar with Scout's brother Jem, their Negro housekeeper Calpurnia, and their daddy, Atticus Finch. He was gentle and wise and never raised his voice or his hand. I was sure that Atticus would never leave Alabama for Texas, not without bringing his two children along.

"Doll, wake up. It's me," was what I heard next. *Mockingbird* slid off the slippery comforter to the floor. Nana stood in the light of the kitchen, her apron still tied around her waist. She was whispering: "Doll," and I pulled myself up from the sofa, pushing aside one of the dining room chairs that protected me from the goons and goblins residing there. In the kitchen, I saw that it was 3:35 in the morning, a crazy hour for a child to be awakened deliberately, but a *promise is a promise*, Nana said. We were church-quiet so as not to wake Aunty.

On the table there was a tiny fork. A small bundle rested on a dinner plate, something wrapped loosely in a linen napkin from Henri's. When I unraveled it, out tumbled two lobster claws. I squealed with happiness, and Nana hushed me with a smile, pouring melted butter from a saucepan into a teacup, and handing me a nutcracker.

This was the time I waited for, when Nana rolled down her stockings and slipped out of her scuffed white shoes: Sunday morning, dark and secret and joyous.

I cracked the shell of the biggest claw in two places, and pulled the prize from it, careful to get the small piece hiding in the *thumb*, as Nana called it. Dropping the hunks of lobster into the butter cup, I tasted the first bite off the tip of the baby-sized fork. It was as delicious as I remembered.

"Sweet meat, Doll?" Nana asked me.

"The best," I said with a mouthful. I chewed this wondrous treat slowly.

"How'd the night go, Nan? Lotsa tips?"

"Not bad. Steady," she told me, patting the apron pocket heavy with coins and paper money.

"Coupla night owls came waltzing in late and stayed until Hank told them to hit the road. They left me a nice piece of change."

We cleaned up the mess together. Nana wiped down the table and I dried it off with a dish towel so it wouldn't wet the newspaper.

Nana plunked down the big Sunday paper like it was a 50 lb. carp, and I gleefully pulled back the funnies from the top; soon, I was reading, in color, *Brenda Starr, Star Reporter* on my belly on Nana's kitchen floor, in the hard white light from the stove.

That's where I was, happy, on the bleached-clean linoleum floor, when I fell back to sleep.

Missing "It"

Twig quit the all-meat diet.

"A person can eat only so much *creature,*" she explained. "If I never see another slab of bleeding beef, it won't be too soon. I'm going the vegetarian route."

That vow lasted a little bit longer than a monarch butterfly in a pickle jar. Apparently, bacon does not grow on a vine.

The summer rolled in brutally hot and horribly humid, and the entire month of July was as sticky as taffy. People were ugly with the heat, rioting in Harlem on a grand scale, according to Mr. Cronkite, and just plain cranky elsewhere. Twig's mood turned black with the rising mercury.

Of course, *working* for a living had her nose out of joint plenty. Her "nest egg" was depleted by mid-June. She began her "career" as a saleslady in the pet department at Kresge's. She arrived home from work on the 5:15 bus rubbing her temples.

"Chirping and squawking and shitting. I'm surrounded by it," she moaned.

"Not much different from *my* life," Aunt Annie told Twig as she poured them each a glass of Schlitz beer. Since Twig had begun her job, Annie watched Arlene and me. Her own baby Martin was too little to be much trouble yet. He slept in Arlene's old bassinette during the afternoon.

I had a fever and a sore throat, so I was saved from eating Aunt Annie's tuna casserole. I sat on the cool kitchen linoleum that looked like a braided rug, playing Barbies. Martha Farrell left her Ken and her Barbie's convertible car last time we played together. When I undressed Ken, he had a strange roundness between his legs that wasn't really a penis. I turned him over to see where the word *Mattel* stood up in raised letters on his pink butt.

I dressed the dolls in their nicest clothes. While I was pulling a skirt up over Barbie's hips, I took a good look at her. She looked a lot like Mrs. Kennedy, with her brown bubble cut. I slipped Barbie and Ken into the convertible.

I was only half-listening to these two women. Aunt Annie was really my mother's best lady friend, not a blood relative. Frank never did like her, and when he was still part of our lives, she had to make herself scarce by suppertime. Now, she could linger as long as she liked. Her own husband worked the night shift at the Ricki Bra factory; she could drink beer with Twig till the cows came home while Tony made certain all the 38 double Ds said so, on the tags sewn inside.

..."it's been so long now, I can't remember when, Annie. Know what I mean? I'll be rusted shut by the next time," I heard my mother say.

"You're not missing much, Twig. Every time Tony comes poking after me, I pretend I'm sleeping," Aunt Annie answered.

My mother let out a snort, her mouth full of sudsy Schlitz. "I guess a woman doesn't miss it until it's gone," Twig mused.

On the floor, I made the plastic car move slowly along the circular pattern of the linoleum. I placed a small green Army man, the one with the tiny plastic rifle molded into his hands, on the tray of Arlene's high chair.

"But if you're really getting lonesome, Twig, there's always Tony's pal Skip. He thinks you're cute as a bug," Annie said between muffled belches.

I pushed the convertible past the high chair, making Barbie and Ken wave with one hand each.

"That would be one big bug he finds so cute. Annie, I swear I wasn't meant to go through life as a nun. I miss having a warm body next to me, one that doesn't belong to a scared kid crawling between my sheets during a thunderstorm." Twig sipped on her beer thoughtfully.

"I've been sitting around long enough. Set something up, Annie. It's now or never, I suppose. Just make sure he has some sort of ass to speak of," Twig declared.

I made a *bang bang bang* noise.

"The president's been shot! The president's been shot!" I whispered loudly. Twig drained her glass and looked past Aunt Annie, out the window, in what I assumed to be the general direction of Texas.

Ho Ho Ho

Twig's calendar was marked with all sorts of cryptic notes. The one date I knew would be circled long before her No.2 pencil even met the paper was July 25, the day when Frank's relatives appeared every summer to celebrate "Christmas in July."

Frank's sister Madeline insisted on this foolish fake holiday. She and her tribe spent most of December in Miami each year, so they forced Christmas down our throats in summer. This might've been a nifty idea, if only Aunt Madeline gave good presents. Instead, she dragged her usual lousy haul up the front steps.

This year, Madeline was teaching ceramics in her basement, which became obvious as we unwrapped useless statues fired in screaming colors. Every year it was some new career for Madeline: real estate, antiques, hair-dressing. This year? Ceramics.

When I turned over my glazed black cat with the neon-green eyes, I read the name *Eunice Fielding* on the bottom.

"Who's Eunice? I think I got her present," I told Aunt Madeline. She blushed and said:

"Mary Katherine, this piece was designed and fired by a famous sculptor."

"Famous my ass," Nana whispered into my ear. "One of her sorry students made that hideous thing and forgot to pick it up after class, I'd just betcha."

Twig unwrapped a big polka-dotted mushroom painted baby blue and school-bus yellow. The day *after* Christmas in July, I took it out back and tried my best to send it over the fence into the Dirty Block by whacking it mightily with one of Frank's old golf clubs. It burst open like an Easter egg, but nothing came out.

"Hey, Vernice, look! Empty as Aunt Madeline's skull," I yelled up to the second-floor window.

"Don't call me that," she warned, "and don't make a mess back there."

Worse than the crappy gifts was spending time with Madeline's two daughters. The cousins simply had nothing sensible to say. Daphne was my age; she had huge spaces between her teeth. When she talked, I couldn't listen because I was too busy staring at those teeth. And her voice drove me nuts.

She talked so soft, I'd have to say: "*Huh?*" one hundred times during a conversation.

The other cousin was Barbara, but Madeline called her *Barbie.* She was about as far from Barbie as she could be, 13-years-old and all pale baby fat and stringy hair. She babbled about horses day and night. Her boring horse talk sent me over the edge, and when no grown-ups were within ear-shot, I breathed in her ear: "Who gives a shit, Barbie?" which prompted a squealing Miss Barbara to rat me out to Madeline. For my effort to stop Barbara's prattle, I received a backhand across my temple from Twig. But it was a lame cuff, mostly for show.

Nana tolerated Madeline and her family even less than I did. She called Madeline "Queenie."

"Royalty has arrived," she announced when their car pulled up.

The big moment this Christmas in July came when Madeline's husband Roland had his fourth highball and told all the kids that he saw Santa on his way to the seashore, lying dead in his crumbled summer sleigh, a Cadillac convertible, apparently the victim of a horrific car crash. This didn't bother me much, because that whole Santa myth had been decimated by my snooping years ago, and poor Arlene wasn't bothered by it. She was oblivious to such things, but I had to soothe her when Roland tried to give her a kiss. She pushed him away like week-old egg salad.

"Could Roland be a bigger jackass?" Nana asked my mother. In the pantry where they'd gone to freshen drinks, they whispered about the one thing about which they saw eye-to-eye, both suffering from the curse of the Hateful Sister-in-law.

Nana liked to say that Aunt Madeline and Aunt Blanche had a lot in common, "no style or substance," was how she put it. With her bragging, breathy ways, nothing about Madeline was true. She burned the brown right out of her hair with peroxide so that her head looked like a bale of yellow straw. She wound it into a French twist and clipped it tightly with a rhinestone barrette, and minced around painfully in high heels that didn't do much for her meaty calves.

Aunt Madeline and Uncle Roland were mean and miserable to each other under their own roof, all smiles and hugs in front of the world. I knew this from staying at their house for a weekend.

I didn't choose to visit there on my own; when Twig lost a baby not long after Arlene was born, my father told me to pack a few things and get in the beach wagon. Two nights and three days of Daphne's whispery nonsense and Barbara's My Friend Flicka talk made my whole head hurt, even my teeth. I was more homesick than I'd ever been in my life, and when Roland discovered the checkbook and started barking about money, I began to wonder just how late the Regional Transit Authority buses ran.

"Spend, spend, spend like a fuckin' Rockefeller! What do you think, I'm *made* of the stuff? Since when do you need a cleaning lady? Get off your fat ass and dust some of this shit yourself. You must have a screw loose, Madeline, if you think this is gonna keep up," Uncle Roland boomed.

Madeline didn't want him showing his true colors in front of me. There was no love lost between Twig and Frank's sister, and Madeline didn't want me to head home with an earful for her sister-in-law.

She worked hard to calm him, but the more she tried to unruffle Roland, the more aggravated he became, until finally he smashed a ceramic figure of St. Francis of Assisi into 80 million pieces.

"Better call your maid to sweep it up, Miss Vanderbilt," he snarled at my aunt, just before he snatched a bottle of *Jim Beam* from the liquor cabinet and closed the door to the study behind him.

I'd never been to a house with a *study* before. There were books lining shelf after shelf in that room, many with the words "abridged" and "Reader's Digest" embossed on their spines, but they had an inch of dust clinging to them, so I knew nobody actually read them. Knowing Madeline, they might have been fake books, hollow, like the ones you could get with Life Savers in them. Miss Harper Lee's name was among the missing in Roland's make-believe study.

There was one extra package in Madeline's sack that Christmas in July, one guaranteed to mortify me and bring a smile to her pancaked face. The tag read: "For Baby Arlene and Molly," and inside were two matching sundresses with hats. Just what I wanted: at ten-and-a-half, to be dressed like my diaper-filling baby sister.

"Over my dead body," I told Twig. Barbara and Daphne smiled twin smiles at the thought.

Of course, I'd done them dirty, too. When Twig and I went shopping at Kresge's for their gifts (taking advantage of her 10% employee discount) it gave me great delight to choose items I knew they'd hate. Because Barbara dreamed she'd one day rise to the lofty position of stable hand, I talked Twig into a nice little play make-up kit, with pink plastic combs and a hand mirror that was really just silver sticky paper instead of glass. My mother knew next to nothing about Madeline's likes and dislikes, and she knew even less about her smarmy kids. I told her: "Barbara will just love it!" For Daphne, I suggested a book about planets. This was sure to bomb, since Daphne was too much of a dunderhead to read anything.

The planet book went over, according to Nana, "like a fart in church," and she patted me on the back when my mother reacted with surprise over Daphne's displeasure. I wouldn't broach this chicanery in Confession. I didn't even know what category this sin would fit into.

"I don't understand," Twig wondered aloud. "Molly picked it out herself."

"Go figure," Nana said as she lit up one of Twig's L&Ms. After a long drag she asked: "How *do* you smoke these things?" but Twig just pretended not to hear.

Roland and Madeline and their horrible offspring managed to leave without ever mentioning Frank's name.

"I just know that he's kept in touch with her. She's hateful enough to keep it from me," Twig groused over a highball. Arlene gagged on a strip of stale ribbon candy Madeline left on the coffee table, and Nana whacked her back hard enough to send the sugary shard halfway across the kitchen.

"There's one gift left, Doll," Nana said, watching my attempts to spin the ceramic cat on its head.

"No sir, Nan. This work of art is all. And don't forget those matching dresses," I reminded her.

"There might be a little somethin' in the long closet," she hinted. Puzzled, I went to my mother's room and dragged the chair to the pull-chain ceiling light inside the closet. The bare bulb swayed as I surveyed the contents; I played in this closet often, and knew everything in it. In a corner by Twig's umbrella, there was a box wrapped in Christmas paper. I brought it out into the bedroom where Nana and Twig stood in the doorway, watching.

I nearly fell off the bed from the happiness of it when I unwrapped a Kenner Give-A-Show Projector. This was so unexpected, I was speechless. To rate gifts, you must realize that Colorforms, with the plastic pieces that made up Yogi Bear and Boo-Boo, was a nifty present. This, however, was on par with, say, an Easy-Bake Oven, the kind of toy you put yourself to sleep fantasizing over every night.

"Who?" was all I could muster.

"I saw it on sale, Doll. Thought you might like it," Nana said.

Thought I might like it! I'd spent many an afternoon staring at this very toy on the shelf at Sid's toy store, lingering in the aisle till his crabby wife Mrs. Sid threw me out. This was enough to send me breathing into a paper bag.

In no time, we'd set up a theater inside the long closet, hanging a bed sheet on one wall as a screen. When I discovered that batteries were required, I began to moan, but Nana produced a handful of them, smiling her HA-HA! smile.

"I came prepared," she laughed, as we made ourselves comfortable in the sweltering-hot closet, munching busted-up ribbon candy, watching grainy film strips of *Huckleberry Hound.*

Twig put Arlene down for a nap and poured herself a third rye and ginger. I thought I heard her mumble something about having a date that night, but I just didn't care enough to listen.

Little Witness

Skip Darnell rang the doorbell twice. Not once-and-then-wait, like ordinary people, but *twice*, right off, as if he was announcing to those inside that someone mighty important had arrived.

Nana went home after two eyeball-numbing hours of closet cinema. Aunt Annie came over shortly after, to help Twig primp for her big re-entry into the world of dating. Twig was a little tipsy by then; her nerves had driven her to it, she claimed.

She'd chosen a seersucker sleeveless shift to wear for this gala event. It was lime green and purple plaid, "quite summery and light," she remarked as she stepped unsteadily into it. After smoothing the dress over her hips, she slipped her feet into white pumps.

Annie's job was to arrange that ever-teetering pile of hair attractively. But Twig's hair defied gravity, and Annie had to shellac it with half a can of *Aqua-Net* to keep it from looking like the Leaning Tower of Pisa.

"Hurricane Diane couldn't move this 'do," Aunt Annie declared.

"Let's just hope he doesn't want to run his fingers through my hair. I'll have to cart him off to the emergency room for stitches," Twig giggled. I knew then that the rye was taking over: Twig was no giggler. Her laugh fit more comfortably under the heading of "Guffaw."

Annie opened the door for Mr. Darnell, which is what I was supposed to call him, since that's the way she presented him to me.

"How'dja do?" he asked me, pumping my hand like he was drawing a bucket of well water.

"Okay," I answered, deliberately leaving off the "And you?" part that Twig had drilled into me. I didn't give a fig about Mr. Skip Darnell's well-being. Twig's eyebrow went up and stayed there.

"Well, hello Mr. Skip," my mother drawled, in a voice that might as well of come out of Jerry Mahoney, it was so unrecognizable. I looked around to see where it came from.

"Twig Medavoy. The world became a lucky place when old Frank took a powder," Skip tossed back with a wolf whistle.

My face screwed up like I smelled one of Arlene's diapers.

"Scoot, Molly," Aunt Annie said. I stayed put.

Skip was a big hairy fellow, bigger than Twig, and wider. His hair was shiny-wet-black with Brylcreem, but for a streak of white that ran through it skunk-like, and I thought I picked up the scent of Aqua Velva when he turned toward the door. I heard Aunt Annie and my mother discussing him one night. Annie said he drove truck for the Telegram & Gazette.

"Steady worker. Not a millionaire, but no loafer, either," was how she put it.

"Shall we?" Skip asked my mother, offering her an elbow.

My mother took his arm. Before she left, she turned to me and urged good behavior. Or else.

"Listen to Aunty. No late-night reading," she told me.

"Goodnight, Vernice," I piped.

"Don't call me that," she warned, but in a sing-song voice, sounding for all the world like a Southern belle.

As soon as the door closed, I began my vicious impersonation of Mr. Skip Darnell.

"How'djadoo?" I bellowed.

"Cut the crap, kid. Your mother deserves some time out," Aunt Annie scolded, but her lips fought hard to avoid a smile.

"Skip's no buddy of mine," I declared before cramming a whole Little Debbie oatmeal cookie into my mouth.

Aunt Annie didn't last much past the *Patty Duke Show*. A couple of bottles of Schlitz and she was snoring with drool running out the corner of her mouth. Baby Martin and Arlene slept solid, even when I opened the squealing bottom drawer of my bureau to get a nightie.

I cut up a dozen issues of Tiger Beat magazine with pictures of the Beatles inside. I planned to make a collage with them, something I learned from the art teacher last spring. Deborah and Martha both had wild crushes on Paul McCartney, and plastered their headboards with his face. Myself, I had a thing for John Lennon. He seemed like a wise apple, the kind of guy who probably "asked for it" as a kid.

Twig wasn't so crazy about their music, though she watched them on *Ed Sullivan* with me last February. She sat through the jamoke with the spinning plates on sticks, but she'd just as soon spin the dial on the boys from Liverpool, she said. She still got all dewy-eyed over Frank Sinatra.

When I was through carving up Tiger Beats, I opened *To Kill a Mockingbird*. Back in the sleepy town of Maycomb, Alabama, Calpurnia just invited Scout and Jem to attend services at her church. There was so much about Calpurnia that was loving, and toward two children who weren't her own flesh and blood, or even the same color. Calpurnia had a grace that made my eyes water whenever she came onto the page.

I tried to follow what Walter Cronkite had to say about civil rights and President Lyndon Johnson as much as I could. It seemed like children of color made up less than 1% of our school population, so I wasn't very familiar with injustice on a grand scale. To me, injustice was the unavailability of sugar cones at Smithfield's Dairy. I had a lot to learn, and Miss Harper Lee was my first instructor.

I'd finished reading this book already, weeks ago, but like always, when I really loved a story, I closed it, opened it and started all over again. The librarian was used to my pattern. She didn't even ask anymore, just renewed it automatically.

At ten-and-a-half, I was sometimes in over my head when it came to reading. Often, I re-read books to better grasp the stories. It was in Harper Lee's courtroom that I first stumbled over the word "rape," and sex suddenly became not only forbidden, clumsy and improbable, but dangerous, too.

I struggled with the word first time around, guessing at its meaning, until I yanked the *Oxford American Dictionary* down from the bookshelf next to Twig's old Singer sewing machine. On page 555, I learned that **rape** (rayp) *n.* was "the act or crime of having sexual intercourse by using force, especially with a woman."

This put a whole new spin on the mystery of sex for me. Sex seemed so stupid already. Why get mean about it, too?

The first time I read *Mockingbird*, I very nearly could not finish it. I wasn't able to pick it up for days after Tom Robinson was found guilty of raping Miss Mayella Ewell. The unfairness of it all just choked me, made my stomach seize up and my eyes fill with tears so blinding, I had to put the book away. "Let us close the springs of racial poison," I heard Lyndon Johnson say on the news one night. Maybe in Mr. Johnson's world, I pondered, Tom Robinson would be believed.

I thought long and hard about Atticus, about his heart and soul, and about the heart and soul of Miss Mayella, about how a white woman's word might be taken over a man's because of the blackness of his skin. People do such frightening things to one another to save themselves, I decided.

I was re-reading *Mockingbird* for another reason: I'd fallen crazy in love with Atticus Finch. The fact that he was quadruple my age didn't enter into my fantasy. Atticus was the most perfect male I'd ever encountered in fiction or real life, and certainly the most flawless of fathers. Atticus Finch would never entertain the idea of running out on his two children. His beloved wife passed away and no one could replace her. No problem required deceit as a solution for Atticus. I wanted an Atticus Finch of my own, to show me the way around unlit corners. He was everything that was good and true to me, and I read his story over and over to keep him nearby, should I need a hero anytime soon.

Around 11:30, I made what looked like a sleeping body under my covers by shoving my winter coat beneath the bedding. Aunt Annie was dead-to-the-world asleep on the sofa with the *Tonight* show glowing from the console when I slipped inside the long closet with a flashlight. Our slapdash movie screen still hung from the wall, and I fed *The Flintstones* into the projector.

Wilma and Betty were frozen across the sheet's wrinkles when I heard my mother's key in the door. From where I sat, crouched in the middle of two piles of cold-weather clothing, I could hear muffled conversation between Twig and Annie. After a moment or two, Annie walked into the bedroom I shared with Arlene and lifted Martin from the playpen where he'd fallen asleep. I listened to the sound of the door closing behind her.

I was just about to emerge when I heard the low gruff voice of Skip Darnell in my mother's bedroom.

"Sure is a nice flat you've got here, Twig," he was saying.

What is Skip Darnell doing in my mother's bedroom? I wondered.

My mother's voice shushed him quiet.

"Not so loud, Skipper. You'll wake my girls."

"Didjou have fun tonight, Baby?" he asked in a slurred whisper.

BABY? My eyes popped and blurred from the image of Barney and Fred chasing Dino.

"You know it," I heard her reply.

"Well, the night don't hafta end yet. Come 'ere."

She said nothing. I strained to listen for words, but all I could hear was movement. The clunk of a boot, the squeak of Twig's aging box spring when someone sat on the edge of her bed.

"Let me do that," he mumbled.

Do WHAT? Surely, Twig wasn't UNDRESSING in front of this stranger.

"Let me hang this up so it won't get all wrinkled, Skip," she said.

Where? In the long closet? I killed the power on my projector and sat stone-still, holding my breath. The door opened and she fumbled in the dark for a hanger, reeking of beer. Not finding one, she stuck the garment on a wall hook, or tried to. She closed the door without realizing that her quite summery, light purple and lime-green seersucker shift had slipped to the floor.

"You know, Twig, I just love a full-figured gal like yourself," Skip growled.

He must have a gun, I thought. Why else would Twig take her dress off right in front of him?

"When you mean 'FAT' say it," she whispered.

"I mean no such thing, Baby. I like a woman I can sink some teeth into," he answered. From Twig came a very faint: "Ouch!" followed by: "Stop that!"

But the words didn't match the tone, and the muffled laughter didn't jibe with the warning. They were quiet for what seemed like eons to me, sitting inside that pitch-black closet, until I heard the box spring sing, and Skip Darnell, making a grunting noise that led me to think they might be moving the furniture around.

There seemed to be a whole flurry of activity, and then- nothing. I waited. I heard Twig get up and shuffle over to her bureau, where her ashtray and cigarettes lay.

"Want one?" she asked Skip Darnell.

"Nah. How do you smoke those things? They got no flavor with that filter on 'em. Kinda like usin' a rubber," he said.

"Oh my Christ. Did you?" she sounded panicked.

"Did I what?"

"Use a rubber?"

"Course not. Those things are like rain slickers, Baby. Why kill the thrill, ya know?"

"Get out, get out, get OUT!" was her answer, hissed through her teeth. That jaw was clenched, I could tell. I could hear his boots drop one at a time as she pushed him out the door.

"Can't I at least put my pants back on, Twig?" he pleaded.

"Do it outside," she whispered angrily. I heard the front door open and close, and Skip Darnell's voice shout: "Bitch!" from the hallway.

Twig hurried off into the bathroom, slamming into the coffee table on her way through the living room. She let out a holler, but kept on going after asking no one: "Who put that there?"

I waited until I heard water running, then I sneaked back into my room, kicking underneath the bed the overcoat that stood in as my double. Through my open window, I could see a gauzy summer haze swiping across the moon like a poorly-washed windshield. Lying there, I was fairly certain I'd just witnessed some crime being committed. I just wasn't sure which one was the victim.

Behind Door #1

It took 20 minutes to get Arlene dressed for a walk to the store. She hated clothes more than the potty seat, and I had a devil of a time corralling my baby sister. She was driving me batty, reciting the same words over and over: "Porkchopporkchopporkchop." She heard Twig say we'd have pork chops and apple sauce for supper, and now she wouldn't stop repeating the words, "like one of the parrots from Kresge's," Twig complained.

After much squirming and loud protest, Arlene finally let me pull Madeline's sundress over her head. I did not wear my matching outfit, thank you very much.

I pulled her chubby legs through the holes in her stroller seat and hollered up to Twig for some money. She tossed an envelope out the second-floor window. Inside was 35 cents for a pack of L&Ms,

49 cents for a loaf of *Wonder* bread, and ten cents for me and Arlene to share.

"Get yourself and your sister a little treat," she told me. Even the idea of a *Welch's Fudge* bar couldn't lighten my black mood. Earlier that day, Twig got it in her mind to trim my bangs, and the results were horrifying.

"Twig, when will you stop playing hairdresser on this child?" Aunt Annie asked. She tugged at my once-again-too-short bangs and blew cigarette smoke out the corner of her mouth, so that it missed my eyes but sailed directly into Twig's.

"She fidgeted, Annie, I swear. I told her to stay still, but she moved, and I had to repair the damage," Twig whined.

I'd spent most of my morning trying to pull my hair at the roots, like a Tressy doll. I'd have to avoid the boys under the garage for weeks.

"What'd you use, a cheese grater?" Annie quizzed.

"Very funny," Twig answered. That's when she told me to get Arlene dressed for a trip to Elmer & Bill's.

"Where you headed and what the hell happened to your hair?" Deborah asked me, once I'd pushed the stroller down Hammond. She popped out from behind Chet's Barbershop, where she'd been playing kissy-face with Bernard Ducharme.

Deborah jumped head-long into the world of kissing that summer; she'd kiss a boy until her mouth was swollen and bruised. No boys had expressed interest in kissing me. I was still waiting for my body to arrive at the same place Deborah's was racing toward.

Beneath the garage, she let the boys run their hands over her shirt, too, so they could feel the growing mounds that would be full breasts someday very soon. As summer closed, she saw herself as almost a teenager, with zero interest in playing Barbies. I didn't feel much older myself, since nothing had sprouted beneath my T-shirt just yet. But when she let Bernard Ducharme touch her, I didn't look away. Something about it sparked me, and sometimes, at night in bed, I pretended it was me who was being kissed, and Bernard Ducharme became William Sparhawk, though his pink penis stayed safely inside his Levis.

Arlene's stroller had its own ideas about rolling down Hammond Street. The wheels went this way and that, and cracks in the sidewalk sent it lurching from time to time. Arlene loved the wild ride, hanging over the front of the stroller like a fisherman peering over the side of a boat. I stopped to rest my arms in front of Mrs. Finnegan's house. Mrs. Finnegan was ancient-old, and in warm weather when her front door was open and her screen door was latched tight, you could hear her television blasting *The Secret Storm* so loudly, you'd swear you were sitting on her decrepit divan with her.

I'd been inside Old Lady Finnegan's house. Once, when I was collecting money for UNICEF, she let me in her kitchen while she went to get her change purse. The clock ticked louder than any I'd ever heard, and the whole room stank of the curious mix of burnt toast and rotting lilacs. The heavy yellowed window shades were forever drawn. Twig said Mrs. Finnegan wasn't such a *hermit* when Mr. Finnegan was still alive, and that confused me. I believed that a hermit was a cookie with raisins and cinnamon, and there was little about Mrs. Finnegan that reminded me of such a thing, though her skin might be called *raisin-y*. Mrs. Finnegan was the closest thing to Maycomb's Mrs. DuBose Hammond Street had to offer. I was hoping to discover that, like Harper Lee's cranky Confederate, Mrs. Finnegan was a morphine addict, but I had no way of telling from where I stood.

I told Deborah about the bread and cigarettes and the dime for treats. She tagged along now, hoping to get a bite of whatever I chose from the candy counter. She held open the door to Elmer & Bill's, so that I could backwards-tug the stroller over the threshold. Arlene loved the cowbell that clanged when the door opened, grabbing for it every time.

Inside, after I got the L&Ms and the bread, I lingered in front of the candy counter for so long that Mae growled at me from the other side.

"Today sometime, huh? Christ," she said, lighting her own cigarette. Mae was what Nana called an *old maid*, never married. Like Aunt Blanche, only very different. Where Aunt Blanche was fussy and girlish, there was nothing fussy about Mae. Her hair was short, cut severely into a "Little-Boy Regular," and silver-colored. Mae was the only woman I knew who had her hair cut by Chet Hastings instead of Barky, the lady's hairdresser. Mae's hands were all big bruised knuckles, and I never put money into them. Instead, I put the change on the glass countertop when I asked for a *Butterfinger*.

"Porkchopporkchop!" Arlene squealed when I broke off a hunk for her. She shoved it into her mouth so fast, she started coughing and I had to slap her back a couple of times to prevent her from choking to death on the spot, right there in the middle of Elmer & Bill's.

After much thought, I bought a box of Milk Bottles, the waxy little shapes filled with colored water. I gave Arlene one more teeny bite of my candy bar, and a bottle of green to Deborah.

"Can't I have red?" she whined to me.

"Get your own dime if you want to be picky. Beggars can't be choosers," I told her. It wasn't often that I had the upper hand with Deborah Rice. Sharing coveted treats was a powerful thing.

We chewed the wax bottles and while we walked, she told me all about finding her father's stash of girlie magazines, filled with pictures like the one I'd found under the garage. I still had that crumpled-up picture of Santa's Helper I'd found, in my shoebox of secret treasures. I took it out once in a while to compare my own stubborn chest to the voluptuous flesh of Magda the Elf.

"These women are bare-naked, Molly, boobies out for all the world to see," she imparted. "I stole one of the magazines and gave it to William Sparhawk."

"He must've been happy about that," I said. "Won't your father notice it's missing?"

"You kidding? He's got a million of them. Besides, he can't exactly ask who took it. My mother would crack his head like an egg if she ever saw them."

We decided to walk the lower street, Patton. This road ran parallel to Hammond, but downhill from it. It was the street I could overlook from my back stoop, where the Dirty Block stood.

When we arrived at the big brick apartment building, we paused to marvel at its decay. I knew from watching out my window that the two fat Gagne sisters on the third floor couldn't manage the steps anymore, so they threw their bags of garbage off the back porch, hoping to hit the pails below. Their aim was poor, which was why, in summer, maggots thrived in the far corners of their yard.

Out front, there was no grass left to mow, only dirt, and the windows were smeared with dried egg left over from a Halloween assault. Some were cracked from the rocks that flew into them, tossed by the likes of Sparhawk and Ducharme. Richard Dumphy and his bug-headed half-sister Lorraine lived there; how a boy could show his face with the Dirty Block as an address, I just didn't know.

Wedged between the fence and the building was the discarded third-floor refrigerator. The filthy appliance had been standing in the yard since spring. Deborah and I were considering it, when I said:

"Wonder what trash they left inside?"

Arlene rocked back and forth in the stroller, bored with this stop we'd made, and Deborah squatted down to give her cheek a gentle pinch. Arlene didn't play along when Deborah tried to start up a game of Peek-a-Boo, eye contact being at the bottom of Arlene's to do list. Deborah was working at catching that strange child's attention when I took a few short steps into the yard to see what was inside the old Norge.

I wasn't prepared for what I saw when I tugged on the grimy handle because inside, where the racks used to be, was grubby Richard Dumphy, curled up dead as a door nail.

I backed up, speechless, until I stumbled and pitched right over Deborah.

"Hey, watch it, will ya?" she squawked.

When Deborah stood up, she saw what I saw, and let out a scream that came from deep inside her, a sound so strangled and strange, it scared me as much as what caused it, and the wax fell right out of my open mouth.

His face was blue-blue, and his even bluer eyes were stuck wide open. He died terrified, that Richard Dumphy. Arlene rocked harder, and it was her happy voice I heard, saying "porkchopporkchopporkchop," over and over again.

Defining Moments

Well, thanks to grubby old Richard Dumphy, there wasn't a mother within city limits letting her child play Hide-and-Seek. It seems that's just what he was doing when he got the bright idea to hole up inside the two fat Gagne sisters' abandoned refrigerator, so that nobody would find him first. Nobody but me, that is.

Arlene, of course, was oblivious to what we'd seen, though her eyes did shine when the police cruisers, the ambulance, and the fire engine filled Patton Street. Mrs. Dumphy came flying through the doorway out front, where there was no door anymore, screaming her head off about her *poor baby where is he where's my Dicky?,* wearing bedroom scuffs and a stained housedress so ratty Twig wouldn't use it for anything better than a dust rag. She shoved her way through the swarm of grown-ups surrounding Richard. I couldn't see much of him through all the legs and uniforms.

The two fat Gagne sisters hung over the railing from the third floor, curious about the commotion, but not curious enough to tackle three flights of stairs. Mrs. Dumphy began moaning, and a policeman asked me all sorts of questions about how I found Richard. I told him it was a simple thing, really: I opened the door and there he was. Dead.

Twig and Annie were suddenly among the onlookers, with Aunty carrying a sleeping Martin on one shoulder. Twig was angry that I was anywhere near the Dirty Block. I'd been warned repeatedly about everything from typhoid to lockjaw when it came to the Dumphy residence.

"Mary Katherine Medavoy, how many times have I warned you about... about this *place?*" she scolded, catching herself before calling it "the Dirty Block" outright in front of Mrs. Dumphy.

There was no *Mr.* Dumphy to insult. Just the slovenly Shirley, whose loud wailing was drowning out my mother's nagging. Presently, Twig turned the stroller full of Arlene and Wonder bread and cigarettes around, and headed home, saying over her shoulder:

"You'd best be following behind me if you know what's good for you, Missy."

I followed, with Deborah Rice clutching my hand. For somebody who thought she was so mature, Deborah looked very much like a scared little girl. She looked like she might be sick. I stopped walking for a minute to ask if she was okay.

"Did you see his eyes, Molly?" she whispered frantically, squeezing my fingers hard.

"Yes," I replied, pulling loose from her grip and shaking my fingers, "and I'd rather forget them, if you don't mind."

But I couldn't forget them.

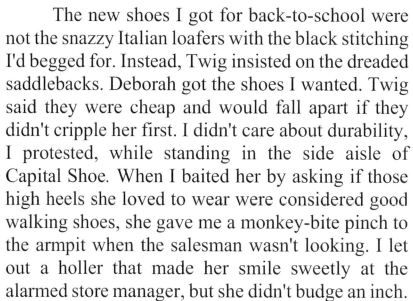

The new shoes I got for back-to-school were not the snazzy Italian loafers with the black stitching I'd begged for. Instead, Twig insisted on the dreaded saddlebacks. Deborah got the shoes I wanted. Twig said they were cheap and would fall apart if they didn't cripple her first. I didn't care about durability, I protested, while standing in the side aisle of Capital Shoe. When I baited her by asking if those high heels she loved to wear were considered good walking shoes, she gave me a monkey-bite pinch to the armpit when the salesman wasn't looking. I let out a holler that made her smile sweetly at the alarmed store manager, but she didn't budge an inch.

On Day One of the 180 days of fifth grade, the sun was in my eyes when I opened them, spilling in through the blinds and over my sleeping sister Arlene, whose arms and legs stretched out wide atop her blankets. Her hair was still damp from the bath she took the night before, and she snored softly as I made my bed. At 6:15, it was already too hot for the first day of school, and the idea of wearing a corduroy jumper and hard leather shoes made me want to climb right back in between the sheets I was smoothing.

"I need a six-letter word for *dumbfounded,*" Twig said to me as I poured my mug of coffee. She was filling in the daily crossword puzzle with a ballpoint pen.

"A-R-L-E-N-E," I answered, and she chuckled without actually looking up.

If the red corduroy jumper wasn't bad enough, the white cotton blouse that went under it was long-sleeved. By the time I got past St. Bernadette's, my clothes were stuck to me. The undershirt Twig insisted I wear for the sake of modesty, felt like a thermal blanket. The only sensible accessories were my white ankle socks; at least my legs weren't encased in tights.

Deborah wore a sleeveless dress of bright orange, with a shiny black patent-leather belt pulled tight around her waist. Her legs looked grown-up in nylon stockings held up by garters. She wore the loafers I'd kill for, and I felt like a baby walking beside her. Somehow, over the long summer, she'd become almost *glamorous.*

Looking at her clothes, watching how casually she wore them, my jealousy was almost too heavy to carry. I tried to chit-chat, so that I wouldn't wind up hating her.

"I was watching the news last night -" I began, but Deborah interrupted me.

"You watch the news? What for? Only finks watch the news," she sniffed.

"I don't know about that," I told her. "I learn a lot about the world watching Walter Cronkite on television. Don't you want to know things?"

Deborah wiped perspiration from her forehead with the palm of her hand, forcing her bangs to stand up like the cockatoo on display at Kresge's.

"Finky," she whispered.

Deborah had the miseries over our placement with no-nonsense Miss Powell. She didn't kid much, especially about her goals as an educator. For Miss Powell, a 55ish bottle-blond spinster with an overbite like Mr. Ed, preparing us for the future was her mission on earth. She'd turn each and every one of us into "productive contributors to society, by God," and to prove it, she piled on homework like nothing we'd ever seen.

It was a curious thing about Richard Dumphy dying over the summer: suddenly, everyone was

Dicky's favorite playmate. The truth was, nobody ever played with him in the schoolyard during recess, and if you had to sit beside him during class pictures, you surely scooted as far to the opposite side of your chair as possible, until the kid on the other side squawked about being crushed, or the photographer got mad. Just because Richard Dumphy finally got a new shirt and a plastered-down little boy's regular for burial didn't change the fact that we never gave him a fair shake. It seemed a little late to try to make up for calling him "Stinkbomb." Richard Dumphy had to die to make friends, and *that* was the truth.

 I'd been dreaming of him regularly; rather, I'd been dreaming of his smelly tomb. In my dreams, I opened the fridge again, but each time, someone different was inside the Norge. I tried my best to shake these dreams; the scariest so far was when I opened the door and Arlene was on the other side.

 Patrick Whelan, whose father owned and operated Whelan Funeral Home, told the grisliest dead Richard Dumphy tales. It was Patrick's contention that he'd sneaked down into the drawing room at night and touched Richard in his casket.

 "I swear he said my name," said Patrick. He added: "We were best friends, you know."

 Patrick Whelan was a liar. He didn't have any more friends than Dicky Dumphy, because he was a blowhard, like his old man. At least dead Richard had dirt as an excuse for his lack of popularity. Patrick was not lucky enough to smell bad.

Once, during fourth-grade Language class, we had to write about our dad's jobs. I wrote all about Frank being a famous fighter pilot and a part-time lion tamer. Miss McDonald called my mother about my "active imagination," and I stayed after for two days washing blackboards as punishment for "deliberate embellishment." Patrick read his essay in front of the whole class.

"My father is an undertaker. This means it's his job to preserve and bury dead people," he began.

The idea of removing blood and replacing it with chemicals was like a horror movie, and when he got to the part about combing dead hair, well, I thought Susan Dorsey would faint. She sat right in front of me, and when she turned around, her face was the color of Aunt Madeline's *Frosted Ice* white lipstick.

Miss Powell's classroom was moved upstairs to the second floor over the summer months, to make room for an extra third grade, and the furniture from storage would be ours. On the very first day of school, despite the heat and our fancy new duds, she told us to clean these desks with *Bon-Ami* cleanser before she'd issue new boxes of crayons to replace last year's peeled wax stumps, snapped and worn from vigorous coloring.

I swirled the grainy powder with a wet rag; Miss Powell assigned me a desk that was once Richard Dumphy's. The Bon-Ami got rid of the crayon marks, but nothing could erase where he'd carved his name. He'd dug his initials into the wood dozens of times, probably while the rest of us were memorizing the seven continents.

When Miss Powell asked who read books over the summer vacation, I raised my hand. When she asked for authors and titles, it seemed as if all the girls read *Nancy Drew* or *Donna Parker* mysteries. Only a few boys raised their hands, and they read *Hardy Boys* stories. I was almost afraid to say I read *To Kill a Mockingbird;* I felt like a colossal oddball.

Miss Powell looked at me as if that's just what I was, when I mentioned that Harper Lee was a woman, remarking: "What a coincidence, Mary Katherine! That's the same book I read this summer."

I felt everybody's eyes on me, then. Thankfully, Miss Powell moved on to the boy next to me. When her back was turned, Deborah kicked a note across the floor to me. I snatched it up and when I unfolded it, I read the word: "FINKY."

"Finky" is what she called me when I got 100% on the spelling quiz Miss Powell sprung on us to test our memories since 4th grade. I was tempted to offer the wrong answer deliberately the next time she called on me, but I couldn't bring myself to say that the capital of California was anything other than Sacramento. More misery awaited me when she asked me to recite the times table for the number 12 and I did so without error or effort.

During silent reading time, I was bored-to-paralyzed by a simpleton's story about Pocahontas, assigned to measure our comprehension skills, so that Miss Powell could figure out who went where during reading lessons. I was finished with the questions at the end before most kids were done with the story, so I mosied over to the gigantic classroom dictionary Miss Powell kept in the center of her reading table. Miss Powell treated reference books like they were the Dead Sea Scrolls. I turned the pages gingerly, until at last I came upon the word I'd been wondering about for weeks:

> **rub.ber** (**rub**-er) *n.* 1. A tough elastic substance made from the coagulated juice of certain tropical plants, or synthetically. 2. an eraser. 3. A person who rubs something, a device for rubbing things.

These explanations made little sense of the conversation I'd overheard from the long closet, the night Skip Darnell got pushed out the door half-dressed. I was still pondering these definitions when Miss Powell realized that I was using the BIG dictionary during silent reading time. Thinking I was looking up a word I didn't understand from the Pocahontas-John Smith love story was enough to send her over the moon with teacher happiness.

"Class, please take note: Mary Katherine Medavoy is using the dictionary to look up an unfamiliar word. That's how we build our vocabulary muscles, boys and girls," she announced to everyone, beaming like a lighthouse.

I'd sunk far into The Land of Finks; I'd likely die there now. From the back of the room came smacking-wet kissing noises.

My face was burning with embarrassment when Miss Powell did the one thing I really hadn't counted on at all: she asked me a question I couldn't answer.

"Mary Katherine, dear, tell the class, would you? What word stumped you?"

My breakfast flirted with the idea of rising up and returning. I flipped the reading-book pages to stall, drawing a big blank. There wasn't one word I didn't know; I'd have to be a moron if this baby book stumped me. Even dead dumb Richard Dumphy wasn't dumb enough for these pages.

"Actually, Miss Powell..." I cleared my throat, stalling some more. "Actually, I was looking to see if the dictionary gives the same pronunciation for the Indian princess's name that we use."

Judging by the groans rolling in from the back rows, I was pretty sure I was as good as dead come recess. I'd be lucky if Richard Dumphy's lice-ridden sister Lorraine played tag with me. By the time we walked home in the patrol line, led now by our new leader Spanky Hooks (whose Christian name was Andrew) I'd had quite enough of 5th grade, enough to last me a lifetime, and that's what I told Aunt Annie when she asked: "How'd it go, kid?" It was then that I realized I was in danger of turning into Scout Finch.

After I finished the mountain of homework Miss Powell assigned to review how stupid we'd become over the summer months, I changed into junky clothes and went outside to the garage, where Deborah agreed to meet me. When I got there, she was sitting on a rock that had the word "ASS" scrawled across it. It was the rock we called "Bum Rock" because it was shaped just like a big butt, crack and all. She scootched over to make room for me.

In her pocket, Deborah had Polaroids from her family's trip to Hampton Beach in August. I wished with all my heart that I'd gone along, because Hampton Beach, New Hampshire was the image I called upon to lull myself to sleep some nights. That's how much I loved it.

I loved its cheesy arcade and its freezing-like-ice water. I loved its playground and boardwalk, and the very smell of it, that hit my nose when the car crossed the bridge from Salisbury, Massachusetts and turned into the Granite State. I loved the stultifying heat of the Skee-Ball alleys, where I could win tickets good for valuable prizes - ashtrays shaped like lobster claws and *Superballs* that bounced higher than the second-floor windows. I could conjure the smell of fried dough dusted with powdered sugar, the taste of it, too, if I concentrated hard enough. The Rice family went every summer, for a whole week, while we went once in a blue moon when Frank's car would make it, and not at all since he "went west."

"Hey, you're Teacher's Pet, huh? How finky can you get?" Deborah asked while I poured over snapshots of my Utopia.

"There's no sin in being smart," I told her, repeating what Aunt Annie told *me* when I whined about my day. "I can't imagine not wanting to know new stuff. I have room enough in my head for all of it."

"Not me," she said with a grin. That I believed.

"Man, it's hot out," Deborah complained, pulling up her shirt to fan her stomach. She wasn't wearing the white lace bra she usually wore under shirts that showed her breasts right through. I could see her nipples when she waved the cotton cloth of her shirt.

"Deborah? What's it feel like, kissing boys?" I asked suddenly, surprised by the sound of my own voice.

"Well, the boys usually get all sweaty, but not me. It's nice, I guess. I think they like it more than I do," she confided.

"But other times," she said, lowering her voice, "It's like my heart is beating in my underpants."

She gave her shirt a big wave then, big enough to fully expose her growing breasts, and I realized she wasn't looking at me, but past me, instead. When I turned my head, the eyes of William Sparhawk were open wide, taking in the show surely meant for him. I left them there, oblivious to the fact that I'd gone anywhere.

I tugged open the screen door and came into the kitchen where Aunt Annie was pouring herself a rye-and-ginger. Twig was home early, she informed me. I could hear my mother throwing up in the bathroom.

Brush Strokes

Twig threw up a lot. It seemed like she was forever munching on Saltines to make the "queasies" go away. She threw up so much, I started to wonder if she was dying.

Death was a big theme for me in the fall of 1964. I was constantly worried that I might wake up dead, or that Twig might choke on a fishbone. It could happen. Richard Dumphy was running around all scabby and repulsive one day, blue and lifeless the next. If the president could get his brains blasted all over the back seat of a convertible, what made me think I was too special to buy the farm?

My attention turned temporarily from the morbid to the magnificent when the new art teacher arrived at our school. Miss Anita Ravelli was everything I'd ever hoped to be, and too good to be true.

Miss Ravelli blew into Miss Powell's fifth grade like a zephyr across the Sahara, bringing high-voltage energy and technicolor to our dreary black-and-white world. A first-year teacher with high hopes, she dressed in *kaftans*, with her glossy black hair pulled back smoothly into a bun. Large gold hoops dangled from her earlobes. Miss Ravelli looked like a page out of *National Geographic.*

She spoke of light and color the way Twig described chocolate: with a reverence most people reserved for religion. She passed out the good white construction paper that made my heart jump when I felt it in my hands, and began teaching the joys of watercolor. I was in love.

She was like a movie star, wearing capes instead of coats, and leather boots even when there was no rain. When she walked into our classroom, Miss Powell's voice faded out like a car radio under a bridge.

Maybe cursive handwriting wasn't my specialty, but drawing and painting were. Every Tuesday, creamy pastel sticks and paint pots drove me to the edge of ecstasy. For "Occupation Day," I penned a composition about my wish to be an art teacher someday. It was the only job I could imagine, having my hands in cool clay, and shading my drawings with charcoal sticks. I wanted to smell like Miss Ravelli, paint and perfume all mixed together, earthy-sweet.

Miss Ravelli told me I was "a natural." I painted vases of flowers and the back of Patrick Whelan's head; I created imaginary sunsets over the vast plains of Texas, and recalled the thundering surf of Hampton Beach with my brush.

Miss Ravelli was thrilled. After three weeks, she pulled Miss Powell aside to tell her that I'd been chosen to paint in the sixth annual *Uncommon Art Festival*, which would soon begin its week-long run on the City Hall Common. This was more attention than I could fathom.

By the Friday before the art festival, I still hadn't thought of a subject, though I'd already painted a bowl of fruit during class that would be displayed on the Common. Nothing had snagged my imagination as yet, and I was hoping something would, and soon.

Come Monday, I was all ants-in-the-pants about painting for an audience. I could barely eat breakfast, and when I did, I felt it all coming back. I had to fight Twig for the bathroom, which was fast becoming a vomitorium.

"You'll do just fine," Twig assured me, as I wretched over the bowl. She was gargling with Listerine again.

A school bus drove all participating students (or "artists" as Miss Powell referred to us) downtown, and Miss Ravelli showed us to the tent reserved just for us. She was a little high-strung herself, and dressed to the nines in the weirdest, wildest robe I'd ever seen. More than ever, I wanted to be Miss Ravelli.

My stomach ached with happiness and terror as we wound our way through the booths, erected beneath enormous green canvas tents by city workers with wrenches in their back pockets and pencils behind their ears.

I wore my best cotton dress, the one with smocking across the chest. It made me look even younger than I was, young enough for adults to feel compelled to rumple my hair, which I hated. Twig tried to trim my bangs for the event, but I protested so loudly, she finally conceded. I refused to paint sporting bangs the same length as my brush, and I told her so.

Behind my seat stood a partition covered with cobalt-blue burlap. Stapled to it over my head was my painting of fruit, all dressed up in a matte and frame, with a tag attached to it, identifying me as the artist and naming my school. Miss Ravelli pinned a *Hello My Name Is* tag to my dress, with the words *Mary Katherine Medavoy grade 5 Hammond Street Elementary* printed on it.

I was a wreck. I hadn't a clue about subject matter, not a single scrap of inspiration.

"I'm not sure what to paint," I told Miss Ravelli.

"Well, set up your paints and try a practice painting, to get the feel for your brush," she suggested. Miss Ravelli was big on "getting the feel."

I nodded, and I did what she said, but I could see that Linda Losapio from Miss Cronin's class was having no trouble in the search for inspiration. She'd already launched into an acrylic of a rider on horseback. Linda was one of those horse-worshippers, like my ridiculous cousin Barbara. Linda collected statues of Morgans and sketched them all the time. Me? I just couldn't see it, this foolish obsession with animals, especially horses. They bored me stiff. Maybe it was the muscles of the horse, so powerful and lean, that she admired. Myself, I'd rather look at William Sparhawk's shirtless back in summer, when he leaned over and didn't see me watching.

I stared at my blank piece of paper.

"Try a still life, Molly. You're quite good at that," Miss Ravelli told me.

That's when my idea took seed.

I lifted the brush and went to work, blending black and white and brown to get the shades of gray I needed. I worked feverishly, once my hands knew what to paint.

Some Hammond Street parents milled around to watch, but I was so absorbed in the mixing and stroking that they didn't bother me a bit. In just a while, I had the vision that had come to my head transferred to the sheet of paper, and I was pleased. Everything was properly proportioned, I believed, and the colors true, the way I remembered.

When Miss Ravelli came to see what I'd created, there was a hush among my audience.

"Mary Katherine, just what is this?" she asked in a nervous whisper.

"A still life," I answered, "Richard Dumphy in the refrigerator."

It was the eyes of Richard Dumphy that most disturbed Miss Ravelli, and elicited a gasp from Linda Losapio. I painted them open, bright blue, the way I saw them when I pulled on the refrigerator door. If Deborah were there, she would've known.

In the next half hour, my paints were packed and my easel folded, and I found myself waiting for Twig to arrive on the number 10 bus to fetch me. Miss Anita Ravelli looked like *she* was going to throw up, and she'd looked that way since I told her what I'd painted.

I wasn't at all sure what sin I'd committed with my paintbrush. Sitting ostracized at the end of a City Hall Common bench, awaiting the wrath of Twig, I knew that Miss Ravelli was no longer the person I most wanted to be. And I vowed never to paint with watercolors again, not until I was an old woman.

Simple Math

In mid-November, Twig announced that there would be no Thanksgiving celebration in the Medavoy house.

"Show me one thing to be thankful for, and I'll stuff a dead bird for you. I can't think of a single reason to bust my hump crushing crackers and mashing potatoes. And I'm not watching that God-damned Bullwinkle balloon float down Broadway, either," she grumbled. I looked up from my oatmeal long enough to give her a sour face.

"Sure. Ruin it for the rest of us," I said.

"What's to ruin?"

Twig's outlook had muddied up back in September, and stayed that way. She'd stopped vomiting, mostly, but her weight was climbing. She no longer spoke of dieting; instead, she ate more than ever. When she wasn't working at Kresge's, she was sleeping on the sofa, and she hadn't plugged in the Hoover upright since Columbus Day.

"I'm worried about Twig," I told Nana. We were raking up the last of those hateful Eurlich leaves, and burning them in the incinerator.

"What's her problem now?" my grandmother asked. Nana saw Twig as a whiner. "I don't know how the hell I raised such a belly-acher."

"She's not quite right, Nana. She stopped making real suppers a while back. We've been eating canned soup and sandwiches for supper lately. She just won't turn on the oven."

"Not much of a loss, Doll. She never was a five-star chef."

"And she's getting...fat, I guess. She's been putting on weight ever since she stopped throwing up," I said.

Nana leaned her rake against the stone wall. She pulled a Lucky from her coat pocket and struck a match, lighting the cigarette inside her cupped hand to keep the wind from extinguishing it. She wet the match head on the tip of her tongue before tossing it over the wall. I watched as she blew streams of smoke from her nostrils, her eyes narrow against my words.

"Was she throwing up in the morning, Doll?" she asked me.

"Mostly. Once in a while she'd barf after work."

We raked the rest of the leaves in silence. Nana had on her thinking cap, for sure. I wasn't sure what the matter was, but something about Twig had her attention. As it turned out, the mystery would unravel soon enough.

When Twig came to collect me on Sunday afternoon, Nana was sitting on the back porch, scraping dog shit from the soles of her old waitressing shoes. She wasn't happy about it, and I had to keep a decent distance, since the very idea of it sent me wretching.

"Whoa. That's one ripe shoe you got there, Ma," Twig said, holding her nose between two gloved fingers. Arlene was snoring in the stroller, her hood tied tight under both chins. Nearly five now, Arlene still preferred the comfort of the carriage over walking anywhere at all. And she couldn't be trusted. Arlene may have inherited Nana's thick curls, but she was not the recipient of her common sense. It wouldn't surprise a soul if she darted in front of a bread truck without giving it a second thought.

"A little queasy, Vernice?" Nana asked.

"Well, goodness! Who wouldn't be, with that horrid smell?"

Nana thrust the shoe in Twig's direction.

"I never knew you to have a weak stomach, Vernice." She stopped scraping the shoe and gave my mother a long once-over, thorough enough to make Twig squirm.

"What are you looking at, Ma? My coat? What?" she asked in a voice full of nervous.

"You. I'm looking at *you*."

From where I stood, I could see my mother's face drain of color despite the cold air. The blood in her cheeks washed right out.

"What's your due date, Vernice?" my grandmother asked. Twig seemed to weave on her feet like a fighter hit by a solid punch.

I never knew time to stand still before this; I always thought that was just a saying in books and movies. But there, on Nana's porch, the world was frozen solid. I watched as my mother regained her composure, made herself stand taller. Each woman locked her eyes on the other, like gunfighters at the OK Corral.

"Springtime. When the swallows return," Twig answered with uncharacteristic defiance.

"Who's the father, if you don't mind me asking?" Nana finished scraping and tossed the shoe across the porch to its mate.

"Why, it's a miracle, Ma. The Immaculate Conception, Part II."

Nana looked vexed now, like she'd grab Twig by that pile of hair if she could reach it.

"Anyone I know? Anyone *you* know, Vernice?"

"None of your god-damned business," Twig told her. I winced. "Get your stuff, Mary Katherine. We're going home."

I wanted to protest and ordinarily would have, but something about my mother kept me from saying a single word. This was no time for wise-cracking or back-talk. I ran inside and snatched up my paper bag.

Outside, I kissed my grandmother goodbye. No words passed between my mother and Nana, and Arlene slept peacefully, oblivious as usual. The walk home was slow going.

That night, I put together the pieces of information I'd collected. Where babies come from, what I heard that night from the long closet, what my grandmother asked my mother - I pulled it all into one big pile. I came to one conclusion:

I was the holder of a secret.

Twig stayed true to her word about Thanksgiving. Nana invited us over for dinner, but I went alone. I missed my mother's stuffing. Nana experimented with chestnuts, sending Aunt Blanche to the bathroom with cramps for most of the evening.

When it was just us two alone in the parlor, I asked my grandmother what it might mean for us if my mother had another baby.

"It'll mean a lot of talk, Doll. A woman doesn't get that way without a man, and no man lives in your house," Nana answered.

"Good thing Arlene will be in kindergarten come fall. Your mother isn't good with chaos. She falls apart like cheap shoes at the first sign of stress."

I sensed I had my work cut out for me.

Birds of a Feather

Twig's boss noticed that she was late to work and early to leave, and slowing down considerably. She went on notice, warned about her job performance.

"Shape up, Vernice, or you're history," Carl Johnson told my mother.

My mother responded to Carl Johnson's threats by stealing our Christmas presents. She took something new every time she worked, small items easy to hide under her wool overcoat, the one with the deep pockets inside. Twig stole pink erasers, and barrettes, colored pencils and a paperback version of *The Miracle Worker*. She became very good at looting Kresge's, but her grandest theft of all was the lovebirds.

Don't ask me how she did it, but she managed to leave work and ride the city bus home with two tiny finches inside her coat. She said she thought they fluttered a tad against her rib cage, but she couldn't be sure. It felt a lot like new life kicking, she said, and she might've been feeling both.

Once inside the kitchen, Twig opened her coat and the birds flew out, confused and rudderless. They whacked into lampshades and sailed into the windows, until I was afraid they'd bash out their teeny brains.

Aunt Annie brought over a bird cage she dug out of the cellar. It was bent in a few places, and somewhat caked with the crud of its former tenants, but Annie cleaned it up to acceptable. She wired the broken door with a bent paper clip so that it would stay shut when you shut it, instead of flapping open. I captured the lovebirds and slipped them into their new home. Twig produced a box of bird seed from her pocket with all the flair of The Amazing Kreskin.

Twig slipped off her shoes and fell into the kitchen chair. I could see where her ankles had swelled up like bread dough rising. "Those birds need names," my mother told me.

I wanted to take my time about naming the birds. They were the only pets we'd ever owned, and I didn't want to choose just any old names for them. I thought a long while before announcing my decision.

"The birds," I told Twig and Annie, "Will be known as Atticus Finch and Gregory Peck."

Both women busted out laughing, hard enough for Aunt Annie to get a noseful of rye and ginger.

"But what if one's a girl?" my mother asked.

"Who cares? That's what I'm calling them. After all, they *are* my birds, right?" I asked.

"You bet," Twig said into her glass, and she shook her head, wondering.

"I don't know where I got that one, Annie. Talk about an odd bird," she said. She looked at me quizzically, like I was a N.Y. Times crossword puzzle she couldn't quite finish.

"What about 'Tweety'?" she inquired. I ignored her.

A week before Christmas, we still didn't have a tree. This fact must've somehow filtered down to Aunt Madeline and Uncle Roland, who shipped us the unexpected: an artificial tree, made of aluminum, complete with a color wheel.

"This belongs in the front parlor of a whorehouse," my mother said as I plugged the tree's limbs into the holes in its trunk. Branch "A" went into Hole "A" with a little coaxing.

"I'd bet that's just where Roland got it, too, that slimy bastard," she added.

Arlene loved the tree. She sat in front of it for hours, staring at the rotation of color that swept across the silver. It was garish and cheap and everything you'd expect from Madeline, but my little sister was mesmerized by it. She'd rock back and forth on her haunches, caught up in the blues and reds and greens.

"I don't know what I'm going to do come New Year's. The child will have a fit when I take that horrid thing down," Twig worried.

Assembled, the tree looked like a bottle brush. Dressed in the box of blue glass ornaments sent by Madeline, it looked like a bottle brush with earrings. My mother refused to hang a single ornament from our own collection. The gold-macaroni-covered styrofoam ball I made in kindergarten stayed safely wrapped in tissue paper, deep inside a box marked "XMAS," stashed in the long closet.

"We'll save that good stuff for a real Christmas," she told me.

"This one isn't *real?*" I asked.

"Not to me," she answered.

Twig had grown more accepting of her situation; she and Aunt Annie spoke about the baby often now. I was curled up on the sofa with a chewed-up copy of *Bambi* by Felix Salten, when I overheard them speculating.

"He's bound to find out, Twig," Aunt Annie said to my mother. The smoke from their cigarettes snaked out of the kitchen like a genie from a bottle. I took a deep breath and tasted L&Ms. "You just know Madeline hears from him. I'd bet dollars to doughnuts he knows you're pregnant."

"Frank Medavoy can kiss my big white Polish arse, Annie. It's none of his business. He saw to that himself, skulking off like the weasel he is."

"Besides," my mother added, "I've never seen any divorce papers. As far as the world and his precious Catholic church are concerned, I am Mrs. Frank Medavoy, and this is Baby Medavoy I'm dragging around."

"Tony saw Skip yesterday." Aunt Annie lowered her voice a notch.

"That so?" Twig's reply was sharp, untrusting.

"He was askin' about you, is all," Annie said with a mouthful of Schlitz.

"Tony didn't tell him, did he?"

"No. At least, not that I know of. Who knows with men?"

"You're lying. He said something, didn't he?" my mother's voice grew pinched and accusing.

"No... I mean, I don't know, Twig. Jesus."

I heard my mother's slippers shift around on the linoleum under the kitchen table. She waited a few moments, until Aunt Annie could no longer hold her lie still on her tongue.

"Well, yeah, he did. He told Skip you were expecting a baby in the spring."

"And?"

Aunt Annie got up and took a bottle of Schlitz from the fridge. She pulled the cap off and poured half into her glass, half into my mother's.

"And nothing."

"Liar."

"Jesus H. Christ, Twig! AND he said he's not worried. It's not his."

My mother was silent. I waited for her reaction, but none came.

"He told Tony he pulled out, that it must be somebody else's," Aunt Annie nearly whispered. I had to crane my neck to hear the last part.

This made no sense. Pulled out? Of what, a parking space?

"That lying bastard! He knows damn well that's not how it went! He's lucky I didn't smash a lamp over his fat head when I realized he wasn't wearing anything."

"Well, it doesn't matter much now. Tony says he quit his job at the T&G and he's headed back up to Canada, where his mother lives."

The kitchen became quiet now. I could hear Hammond Street traffic crunching over fresh snow just outside.

"Good riddance to bad rubbish," my mother said in her lowest voice, and I heard their glasses clink in a toast to the ruination of Skip Darnell.

———◇———

Compared to Twig's man-made mess, the fifth grade was a breeze. Over Christmas vacation, I read three books and wrote a report on Greek gods, but my social life was as stale as last week's Wonder bread. Deborah Rice said she wasn't planning to open a book unless it was the TV Guide.

"You think boys don't like you now? Just keep it up. Honestly, Molly, why are you so finky?" she asked me. We were in her bedroom, thumbing through a ratty copy of the book *Peyton Place*, trying to find the good parts. I'd graduated to steamy novels lately; this coverless copy of Grace Metalious's 'classic' was hiding in Twig's bookcase, between *Pride and Prejudice* and a Massachusetts road atlas.

"You just don't get it, do you, Molly?"
"Get what?"
"What boys like. You don't got a clue."
"That's *'haven't a clue',*" I corrected.
"See what I mean? Finky," she sighed.

The other two books I'd been reading by flashlight were by James M.Cain, *The Butterfly*, and the *Postman Always Rings Twice*. *Postman* was an old movie with Lana Turner in it, and I'd seen it a few times on the *Late Show*. But the thin novel the movie was made from was a whole different ball of wax. For one thing, in the movie nobody was biting each other till their lips were bleeding, and the woman never once got socked in the leg so hard it nearly knocked her over, just because she "liked it like that."

These people scared me, they were so cold, plotting murder as easily as making a grocery list, and I couldn't keep me eyes away from the pages. Deborah would never understand the worlds I climbed into between the covers of books, and truly, I didn't care if she did. She was too stupid, something I'd known all along about her. I would read until my head was full of every conceivable kind of life, and then pick one to live.

That was my plan.

Frank Talk

Gregory Peck and Atticus Finch were not producing the nestful of eggs I'd hoped for, though my mother was well on her way to being fruitful and multiplying. It seemed like every day she grew bigger with baby. Her legs swelled to comical, except that Twig said it was no laughing matter, Missy.

For Valentine's Day I made Twig a beautiful card from red construction paper, Elmer's Glue and cut-up doilies. Inside, I wrote "I LUV U BOTH" and gave it to her while we waited for the coffee to finish perking. Twig cried.

"Thank you, Mary Katherine. I don't know what I'd do without you, somedays."

I wished I'd been able to buy her a bottle of Jean Nate toilet water, but I couldn't scrape up the cash. Money was exceptionally tight; in fact, it was becoming a scary problem for us.

It was Valentine's Day when the phone call came from Texas. I watched Twig's hands shake uncontrollably as she held the receiver to her head.

She listened a long time, saying nothing after the words:

"Yes, this is Mrs. Frank Medavoy."

When she was through, she placed the phone down gently, and her eyes filled up and spilled over. She sat down heavily in the kitchen chair, and lit an L&M with hands that fluttered like tissue paper.

"Your father's dead," she told me.

Aunt Annie came right over when I rapped on her door and told her Twig's news. I poured beer into glasses for both women as my mother told the story of how my father died.

"Seems he was beaten to death by two teenagers. Boys. They wanted his wallet, and he wouldn't hand it over, so they kicked his head in until he let go of it."

Annie gasped.

"I can see Frank holding on to his god-damned money until his last breath, the fool," my mother added, whispering the last two words.

"Are you alright, honey?" Annie asked me. I jumped a little when she turned toward me.

"Me? Oh, I'm fine, Auntie. I was thinking that Arlene doesn't even remember him."

"She doesn't remember yesterday," Twig said.

The whole idea of being fatherless struck me as strange. Despite the fact that Frank had been absent from my life for two years and pretty much invisible even when he *was* part of our family, the thought of not having a father was weird. I rather liked it; it put me in a place I'd never visited before.

Frank's death was like a good news/bad news joke for us. It was bad news to know that your father's head was kicked in, certainly, but good news to know that your husband had a hefty insurance policy. Twig buried Frank conservatively, not wishing to waste precious cash on a fancy box that would be dropped into the ground and covered with dirt.

She settled on a plain coffin for my father, after a terrible row with Aunt Madeline. My mother wanted to cremate Frank's remains, and this notion sent my Aunt into another galaxy.

"No Catholic soul can reach heaven if it's been burned!" she screamed at my mother.

"How the hell can you burn a soul, Madeline? Use your head," Twig calmly replied.

"It's against God's laws!" Madeline pleaded

Twig finally gave in to my aunt's wishes. Nana was amused by the debate.

"As if God made such foolish laws," she chuckled.

"Would that be the same God who said we can't eat meat on Friday or we'll roast in hell? Like a fried bologna sandwich would tip the scales!"

So as not to accommodate Madeline *too* much, my mother refused to hold a wake for Frank. This set Madeline's teeth on edge, since she'd already purchased the perfect black dress at Eddy's on Park Ave. Who would see it now, in February, when everybody knows it's too damn cold to take your coat off inside St. Bernadette's because Father Vail is cheap with the heat? she squawked.

Twig wasn't budging on the subject. Not with a big belly to explain.

"Best you not leave yourself open to close scrutiny," was how Nana put it.

We buried Frank on February 22, 1965, George Washington's birthday. It took a week for the body to be returned from Texas. I never did take a look inside to see if it really was Frank Medavoy's bony little self we were bidding farewell. Twig identified him and deemed him too bashed up for viewing, and his casket remained shut at Whelan's funeral home.

His obituary read that he left two daughters and a wife, a sister and a brother Timothy. I'd never laid eyes on Uncle Timmy in my whole life. He was the phantom uncle, the one rarely mentioned, and in whispers at that. Madeline insisted we include his name in the newspaper's account of the life of Francis Xavier Medavoy, though Twig thought it silly to waste the ink on a man no one ever heard from.

"Why haven't I ever seen Uncle Timmy, Vernice?" I asked, as I struggled to keep a grip on Arlene's left foot. I'd been placed in charge of dressing my sister for our father's funeral Mass, and holding on to her was a lot like trying to embrace a trout.

"Because he's a criminal," my mother answered. "And don't call me that."

"What sort of criminal? Like, a bank robber, or a murderer?" I asked.

"Like none of your business," she told me. "Now hush up with the questions."

Arlene looked reasonably civilized when I was through dressing her. Her hair was impossible to pull a comb through, but I managed to brush it into a ponytail and secure it with a rubber band. It was the best anyone could expect from one person with two hands. In general, Arlene wasn't turning out the way we'd hoped she might.

I'd taken the bus downtown with Nana the day before, to buy a new dress to wear for my father's funeral. Arlene was wearing one of my cast-offs, a tartan plaid wool jumper with a white cotton blouse beneath it. Everything I'd ever owned wound up on Arlene, who couldn't care less about any of it. At

Barnard's, Nana found a black velvet dress with long sleeves and a white lace collar. It was tucked deep inside the sale rack, hidden among the rest of the holiday dresses now selling for one-half off the original prices.

"Gotta know how to look," she explained to me.

On the bus ride home, I tried to pick Nana's brain about Uncle Timmy. Since my mother's cryptic remark, I'd become fascinated with her brother-in-law and the things I didn't know about him. There was only one photo of my father's brother in our album; in it, Uncle Timmy was a boy of my age, standing at the top of a staircase, staring down at the camera. His face wore a scowl, a look of pure dislike for the photographer, for the idea of being photographed, for the world around him.

"Timothy Medavoy was born under an angry star," Nana told me, when I rooted around for answers.

"Will he come to Frank's Mass?" I asked.

"Highly unlikely," she told me.

After I was finished fixing Arlene, I sat her in the rocking chair, dropping a busted Slinky in her lap. She loved to rock back and forth, and would do so without the aid of a chair, but the combination of rocking and watching a Slinky would mesmerize the five-year-old long enough to allow me to get myself ready. It seemed a shame to wear such a lovely dress for such a dismal occasion.

I brought the Slinky along to church. I knew it wasn't right to play with toys during Mass, especially during an event as solemn as your own father's funeral, but Arlene wasn't like other kids. "Hush" had no meaning to the child, nor did the words "stay still." I knew Twig would be grateful I'd thought to stuff it into my coat pocket.

Father DiStefano had a tough time eulogizing Frank Medavoy. Frank wasn't exactly a regular church-goer; more like one of those "half-assed" Catholics, as Aunt Blanche would say. The padre had never really laid eyes on Frank, so the day before the funeral, he'd come knocking at our door for some clues to my father's character.

Twig looked up from the skillet, where she was crucifying three pork chops.

"Well, Father, he had no ass to speak of," she said helpfully.

Father DiStefano coughed. The pork chops sizzled.

"And he abandoned his family to seek fame and fortune in the great state of Texas," she added, an L&M dangling magically from her lower lip. Her belly was so big, she could hardly get close enough to the stove to peer into the frying pan.

"Put those facts into your eulogy, and you'll satisfy me," she said cheerily. The smoke from her cigarette made her eyes squint. If I didn't know better, I'd think she was flirting.

At the funeral Mass, Father DiStefano tap-danced around the fact that Frank deserted us, describing him as a "traveling salesman" in love with the road and where it might take him. He left out that any road leading from our apartment would do. Arlene fidgeted awfully until I remembered that bent-up Slinky, and Aunt Madeline boo-hooed and wailed like there was no tomorrow.

"You'd think she cared, the way she's carrying on," Twig stage-whispered.

On my way back from Communion, I noticed a man standing in the last pew, apart from the other mourners. I knew right away it was Uncle Timothy Medavoy, the boy in the photo album. He was peering up at the ceiling, and kept his eyes there for the longest time.

Burial at St. Stephen's Cemetery was put off by the cold; instead of lowering Frank into the ground, we filed him in the mausoleum the way Mrs. McCracken might alphabetize some kid's attendance records at Hammond Street Elementary. The limousine that carried us there was pretty much done with us. We hitched a ride to the VFW with Aunt Annie.

"Was that Uncle Tim?" I shouted from the back seat. The car radio was blasting the Supremes, and Twig was singing along louder than Diana Ross ever could.

"STOP! In the name of love..." she crooned, ignoring me. Her hair was piled high enough to attract birds for nesting.

"VERNICE!" I bellowed. She twisted the radio volume knob so hard, I thought it might've snapped right off in her palm. Arlene began moaning.

"Don't call me that!" she screeched.

For once, I left it alone.

I searched the sparse crowd at the VFW for Uncle Tim's strange face, but he was nowhere to be found. Nana said that was a good thing, but I couldn't see how. I reasoned that any man who would find his way home to say goodbye to his brother couldn't be all bad.

"Some men just carry the dangerous scent, Molly," she informed me. I wondered if danger smelled like anything familiar.

The cold-cut platters were empty within minutes, and the mourners seemed to have adjusted to life without Frank Medavoy on earth quite comfortably, once their bellies were full. Most sat at the bar, ordering highballs. I heard no mention of my father in the conversations that shot up around the drink orders. I chased Arlene out from under a table, where she'd stashed six pieces of olive loaf and lined them up in a neat row.

This was how the girl played, I'd been noticing lately. She seemed bent on lining things up, everywhere we went. All the shoes in our apartment rested in tight rows now, as did the set of rusty Matchbox cars Nana purchased for 25 cents at a garage sale. Arlene didn't give a fig about the messiness of her appearance, but she kept the world around her organized nicely.

"Yeah, that was Timmy Medavoy, sitting in the back of St. Bernadette's," I overheard Chet Hastings say as I peeled sweaty olive loaf from the tiled floor.

"Hasn't been seen since that trouble back in '56," he added.

"I thought that was Tim. The only good-looking Medavoy in the tribe, even if he is a fire-starter," Lou Hastings commented to her stepping-out husband.

"Well, now, his sister Madeline is a handsome woman," Chet mused.

"That blister? Chet Hastings, you'd screw a snake if you could keep its head still, I swear." Lou's voice dropped into a hiss.

The Hastings seemed to notice me right about then, and the subject of their talk changed to Chet's barber shop abruptly. I knew I'd be seeing Mrs.Hastings slip into the Confessional next Saturday, for certain.

What trouble in '56? I wondered. What was a fire-starter, anyway?

Twig was looking woozy from the rye she'd been sipping.

"Maybe we should head home," I suggested, trying to hold onto Arlene's wrist as she twisted my arm like corkscrew macaroni.

"Not just yet, Molly," Twig answered. She'd been shunned by most of the crowd all afternoon, and talked to only by the women brazen enough to want to gather gossip for hair day at Barky's. Twig was wearing her miffed face, the one where her eyebrows locked together and grew thicker by the minute.

"Not till I have a few words with Madeline."

She stood up unsteadily, and smoothed her dress over her belly as best she could. Twig scanned the room for my aunt, and when she zeroed in on Madeline, she headed her way.

"Madeline. I understand you have something to say about your brother's child."

"Excuse me?" Madeline asked sweetly. She was sipping the Brandy Alexander Chet Hastings sent over.

"Don't do it. I was in the ladies' room stall when you were referring to your niece Arlene as a "retard."

Twig towered over Madeline, her pile of hair growing higher as she raised her chin.

"Why, I would *never*!" Madeline fumbled, but I could tell by the queasy look on her made-up face that she was caught for sure. Twig must've been simmering all afternoon.

"Unless you were talking to yourself in there, I thought for sure I was hearing two voices, and one of them belonged to your daughter Barbie."

"Vernice, you must be crazy with grief," Madeline croaked.

"My little girl is not mentally retahh-ded, or anything else. She just got a good look at her bloodline last time you visited and decided to try a different way."

Twig's voice grew big as her hair.

"And I'd rather have a kid who lines up cold cuts than one who shovels horseshit."

Aunt Madeline's face seemed filled with real feeling for the first time, like some shiny mask had slipped away to reveal what was in her hard little heart. What I saw was what I'd always suspected: something worse than hatred, an emotion made up of equal parts disgust and jealousy.

"You've got nerve, standing by my brother's casket carrying a bastard child, Vernice. You think people can't count? My brother's been gone a long time, and unless you're birthing an elephant, that's another man's baby. You, Vernice, are the trash I always said you were."

I fully expected Twig to split Madeline's lip. Instead, she put her hand on my head gently, and said in a low, tired voice: "Let's go, Mary Katherine."

With everything I had in me, I lifted Arlene onto my hip and carried her out to the car. She was clutching a piece of cheese she'd pilfered, chanting: "Bastid, bastid, bastid," over my shoulder, like a lullaby, and she did so the whole ride home.

Burnt Out

The time after my brother was born seems hazy now, foggy like a dream only not a dream. He was very real, that baby boy, and needful. Twig named him John Fitzgerald Medavoy, after our slain president. Evidently, "Lyndon Baines Medavoy" was not an option. He came into the world with a head covered in curly black hair, and sideburns, like a baby Elvis Presley, on April Fool's Day, 1965.

Twig took to calling him "John-John" which flipped my stomach over. She reasoned that their souls were entwined, our baby and the son of the 35th president, because both of their fathers died in Texas. I knew enough not to remind Twig that John Fitzgerald Medavoy was the unplanned offspring of Skip Darnell. She was in what Aunt Annie referred to as "a fragile state" during those days after giving birth. I was feeling pretty fragile myself, pulling duty as Arlene's shadow.

He didn't sleep much, that John Fitzgerald Medavoy. He was an angry baby, his fists all balled up, his face blue-red more often than not. Aunt Annie christened him "Fitzy," a name that Twig tolerated because of Rose Kennedy's father having the same nickname. Mercifully, it stuck, and "John-John" was no more in the Medavoy house.

His cries woke me nightly, as did the smell of Twig's L&Ms, burning down in the lobster-claw ashtray. I took to creating stories while lying in bed each night.

Arlene's soft snoring never kept me awake like a baby's wail will, but I listened to it now, its rhythm a comfort. Regularly, I imagined Uncle Tim, making up the answers to all my questions about his dangerous past.

Sometimes, I imagined him at our door, happy to see only me. He'd lift me in his arms and kiss my cheek. I pictured his arrival a thousand times, but as spring became summer, my imaginings matured and twisted into something scarier, more thrilling. Sometimes, I substituted William Sparhawk for Uncle Tim. That's when the kiss moved to my mouth from my cheek, and the hug turned into a caress. My own body would resemble Santa's Helper in these dreamy moments. In the sticky night air, I'd kicked away my blankets and flip my pillow over to its cool side.

I woke one night to the sound of Twig searching for a book of matches. Fitzy had only just fallen back to sleep. I walked past my mother to the bathroom when she startled me with a "Hey!"

"Molly! Don't you feel it?" Twig pointed down toward my pajama bottoms. When I placed my hand there, my fingers came up bloody.

It was the miracle of womanhood, Twig explained. The sign we all wait for. I hadn't been waiting to bleed to death, I told her. I had no burning desire to ruin my best baby-doll pajamas, either.

"You're a little young, 12. I was nearly 14, but I think it was my weight that slowed me up. Come with me. We'll take care of this business."

Twig set me up with a sanitary belt and a *Modess* pad so thick I felt like I was walking with a sofa cushion stuffed between my thighs.

The miracle of womanhood left me listless and uncomfortable for days. I didn't like it and I didn't want any part of it, and I said so.

"Time will come, young lady, when you'll be pleased as punch to get a visit from your 'friend.' In fact, you'll someday put out the welcome mat for it," Twig assured me.

'Friend' indeed, I said to myself. I didn't see where anything womanly was happening to the rest of me. My chest only barely swelled from this grand experience. My belly hurt. I looked nothing like Santa's Helper. If all this was the splendid initiation into some exclusive girls' club, I was all for being passed over for selection. This must be the hazing.

"Now can I shave?" I asked. Twig surrendered on this point. Finally, I could do something about the downy layer of dark fuzz that covered my legs. Next victory in the never-ending battle to grow up: the garter belt.

While I may have been victorious in this minor skirmish, there was little I could do about Twig's blind spot when it came to my hair. If the pixie cut she forced on me for the past decade wasn't homely enough, she got it into her head that curls would transform me into movie-star material. I was wooed by her sweet talk on this matter: "Molly, you'll be gorgeous! Grown-up looking, you know? Trust me." My first mistake, and a costly one.

The result of Twig's brainstorm left me with a skull full of over-processed frizz. My already-too-short bangs shriveled up like dead leaves on my forehead, and the horror on Aunt Annie's face was all I needed to see to know that I was officially a sideshow freak.

"I'm never leaving the house again! You can get your own stupid L&Ms from now on!" I shrieked. "I'm never going to school, or church, or Denholm's or *anywhere* ever again as long as I live!"

Twig took a long drag off her cigarette and looked me over with a frown.

"Maybe the neutralizer failed," she mused.

"Maybe I look like Little Orphan Annie!"

Twig studied my burnt-out bubble cut.

"More like Nancy, Sluggo's girlfriend," she decided.

There was nothing I could do about this abomination. I slammed the bedroom door so hard the kitchen clock popped off the wall and smashed on the linoleum. Time didn't matter to me anymore; I'd have to mark the months on my wall like a prisoner ticking off his years behind the bars of Alcatraz. All I could do was wait - wait, and wear hats.

I had an eclectic assortment of headwear to choose from: a Canada Dry baseball hat, a wool stocking cap with a missing pom-pom, a genuine if somewhat beat-up sombrero given to Frank by Roland and Madeline after their honeymoon in Tijuana, and a red bandana.

While I was rooting around in the long closet, searching for more hats to hide my mother's handiwork, I discovered a box from Morse Shoe. It was taped up like Fort Knox, so naturally I was compelled to peel back the adhesive strips until the lid was free. Inside, I found newspaper clippings, neatly cut from the Telegram & Gazette. The word "arsonist" caught my eye.

I knew what this meant. It was a spelling word I'd encountered with Miss Powell. According to the T&G, an arsonist had burned down the campaign headquarters of a local politician. The article said the building was engulfed within minutes, and had been doused with an incendiary liquid, most likely gasoline. The remains of an unidentified victim were discovered by firefighters.

Further rooting got me another clipping, this one with the headline "Arson Suspect Apprehended." The accompanying photo showed a man in handcuffs, his jacket collar partially covering his jaw. I didn't have to read the caption to know I was looking into the eyes of the same little boy who stood scowling at the top of the staircase so many Christmases ago. By then, Uncle Tim had turned the scornful glare into an art form.

I held in my hands the "trouble back in '56," so casually recalled by the Hastings. Evidence suggested that Uncle Tim was involved in an arson for hire scheme, having been recruited by the incumbent mayor himself to destroy an opposing mayoral candidate's headquarters. I sifted through the remaining articles, but nothing in the shoe box told the outcome of Uncle Tim's arrest. I'd have to search elsewhere for the rest of the story.

A victim meant murder charges, that much even I knew. You burn down a building with a human being in it, and you're in a lot more hot water than the punishment you'd get for tossing a match into an empty building. This fact made Uncle Tim a murderer.

This fact made Uncle Tim irresistible.

I placed the clippings back inside the Morse shoebox and carefully pressed the tape back to secure the stash. Not long after, I pulled the Canada Dry baseball cap down over my frizzy skull, and made my way to the public library. Only a week before, we'd learned how to look up newspaper articles in what the librarian called the archives. I spent the afternoon pouring over microfilm editions of the city newspaper, scanning the screen until I finally found what I was looking for: the acquittal of Timothy Medavoy.

I knew what an acquittal was; Atticus Finch had hoped for one in the case against Tom Robinson. And now I knew that Uncle Tim was found to be not guilty of the crime of arson. A good thing.

So why was I disappointed?

Room for Rent

There was nothing to be done about Fitzy's crying. Aunt Annie diagnosed him as colicky, meaning that he could not be soothed by any known method of mothering. Twig walked the floor with the boy for hours on end, with an L&M jammed between her two fingers and a bottomless cup of coffee in the same hand. That's just what she was doing one early summer evening when the front doorbell rang.

"Molly, could you get that?" she asked over Fitzy's endless howl.

Nobody familiar ever came to the front door. I scrambled down the stairs and stood on tip-toe to reach the peephole, and through its fisheye lens I saw the distorted face of Uncle Tim.

I scrambled right back up the stairs.

"Twig, it's Uncle Tim!" I announced, my heart racing like Seabiscuit's. She stopped pacing and stared at me.

"Sweet Jesus. Now what?" she mumbled.

"Well? What should I do? Should I let him in, or what?" I was trembling now.

"Let him in, I suppose. What the hell could he want from me?" she wondered.

My descent was more measured this time, as I placed my feet gingerly on the carpeted steps. The dim hallway was wallpapered formally, and for a split second I felt like Scarlett O'Hara greeting Rhett Butler. That vision dissolved when I spied the pores of Tim Medavoy's nose through the peephole.

"Vernice home?" he asked shyly when I jerked opened the front door.

"Yup. You wanna come in?" I tried to sound casual, though I'm certain my voice quavered.

There was no Hollywood reunion when Uncle Tim walked into our living room. My mother's eyebrow was arched ala Nana from the minute he crossed the threshold, and the only word to accurately describe Frank's baby brother would be sheepish. He carried his hat by his side, and his upturned collar lay limp on one side, as if it had given up trying to look jaunty.

Oh, but he was the handsome Medavoy, the one who got any good looks that floated in the family gene pool, and the air of mystery that surrounded this visit was enough to keep me glued to the braided rug.

"What brings you here, Tim?" Twig asked sharply. I'd never seen her so steely, so unwelcoming.

"Well, first, Twig, I'd like to offer my condolences to you and the children."

"You lost a brother, Tim. I only lost a deserting fool with no ass to speak of," Twig interrupted.

"I understand. Frank had no business leaving you and the girls behind. Is this my nephew?"

I couldn't wait to hear Twig's answer.

"He's somebody's nephew, I suppose. Not yours," she said.

"Oh." I was beginning to feel enormous sympathy for my Uncle Tim. Twig was turning into Nana right before my eyes, and a more formidable opponent he'd never meet. The heavy silence that hung was unending. Finally, I broke it myself, with a loud burp. I couldn't think of anything else to contribute to the conversation.

"Lovely," my mother said, and looking Tim straight in the eye, she added:

"Molly's inherited your sister Madeline's charm."

"Madeline, yeah," he nodded.

"Well, out with it. What is it that brings you back to Massachusetts, not to mention Hammond St?"

"Now, that's a story in itself, but I was hoping to start fresh here, and find work. I understand that times are tight for you and the kids, Twig. I was wondering if you'd want to take in a boarder; that is, a paying one."

I could see Twig's wheels spinning.

"Where would I put you?" she asked, but Tim only shrugged. She dropped a whimpering Fitzy into my arms and began to walk about the apartment. From room to room, she sized up the possibilities as I trailed behind her. Behind me came Uncle Tim, and behind Tim came Arlene, apparently liking the uniformity of such a parade. We stopped at each doorway and peered into the rooms as if seeing them for the first time.

"I suppose I could give you my room and I could bunk in with the girls. It'll be a tight squeeze with the crib in there, but I'm assuming you don't want to live with us until the end of time, hmm?"

"Only until I'm on my feet," Tim answered.

"I won't set my watch by that," Twig replied.

It was settled. Uncle Tim would move in by next Saturday. Because Twig's bedroom was larger, she decided to move us into it instead of the other way around. I hoped the spots where Arlene had peeled back the wallpaper to expose the horsehair walls wouldn't bother our new tenant. I suggested Uncle Tim take my bed instead of Arlene's pee-stained mattress. He agreed, and Twig carted the ruined bedding to the curb on trash day. Bedtime from now on meant Arlene in the middle, and Twig and me on the ends, with the baby's crib jammed next to Twig's side. After one night, the toilet training of Arlene became our main goal.

Arlene had become a handful, alright. She was growing taller, yet no other signs of growing up accompanied that fact. She still preferred her own company, and had no interest in playing with other children from the neighborhood. They kept a safe distance from her, at any rate. She was known to suddenly bounce a rock off a head without warning, and Twig was tired of apologizing to irate mothers whose snuffling kids stood bleeding in our backyard.

"Maybe you should think about …placing her," Aunt Annie suggested.

It was a suggestion made only once. The look Twig gave her made repeating the idea a very bad one.

I knew Annie meant a "home." Someplace for crazy people, like the hospital where they stuck poor Olivia de Havilland in "The Snake Pit." A booby hatch. That was surely no place for my sister, but Arlene would be school age that fall, and not even out of diapers yet. She still didn't carry on conversations like a regular person might, and lately her temper tantrums were difficult to head off. The older she got, the harder it was to decipher her needs and wants. She'd become angry out of the blue, wanting something she couldn't name. I'd run around grabbing items to offer her, like the natives bringing Ann Darrow to King Kong. Now and then, I'd guess correctly, but it was a crapshoot. The one thing I knew for sure was this: she did not like Fitzy.

It wasn't so much Fitzy she objected to, as his crying. It truly sent her into a tailspin. If he was sleeping, she'd pay him no mind, but once his colicky howling began, she'd growl. His constant hollering aggravated the usually oblivious Arlene, who would clap her hands over her ears and rock on her haunches to escape the baby's grating wail. Oddly, the one person who could soothe her was Uncle Tim.

I never heard him inquire about Arlene's condition. If he did, it was out of earshot. He simply accepted her for who she was, and became the only person she allowed to embrace her. Human touch was a thing she could do without, but a hug from Uncle Tim was something she actually sought.

"She's taken a shine to you, Tim," Twig marveled. Arlene sat in the same chair as Uncle, fidgeting with the wristwatch he wore on his left arm. Uncle Tim, I discovered, was a lefty.

It was a rare moment when Uncle Tim was home long enough to sit. He worked all kinds of crazy shifts at Wyman - Gordon's, sometimes not appearing at our supper table for days. Twig washed his uniforms and I hung them to dry on the clothesline out back, where Arlene sat tethered to the pole.

Apparently, any misgivings over Uncle Tim's criminal past were obliterated by the cash he handed Twig weekly. She asked no questions, and bought for him the few items he requested by way of groceries: saccharine for his black coffee, two tins of sardines, packed in oil, and saltine crackers on which to lay the slimy fish before eating them. He ate lunch from the "roach coach," he told Twig, the truck that stopped at the gates of the factory at noon.

Twig was beginning to worry less about Uncle Tim living under our roof. Her mother, however, was not so relaxed.

"Are you nuts, Vernice? He's never been anything but trouble, which you are in no need of, or aren't your hands full enough?" Nana asked.

"Ma, he's not the same as he was. He's lost all that meanness. You should see him with Arlene. She just adores him, and that's something I never say about anybody, myself included."

Twig lit an L&M, sucked it in and tilted her head back to exhale. She was making a valiant attempt to appear unnerved, but I knew better. I was belly-down on the kitchen floor, trying to fish the ace of spades out from under the refrigerator with a coat hanger, and I could see her left leg moving to beat the band.

"Molly, what's your opinion of the man?" Nana startled me with this question. In my entire life I'd never been asked my opinion of anything.

I sat up, coat hanger in hand. Attached to the hook was a ball of what Twig called "kitties," dirt and dust from what could have been the Eisenhower era. Slowly, I pulled from it a plastic cowboy and an ancient throat lozenge.

"He's nice enough," I answered. They looked at me, waiting.

"Are you asking me if I think he'll burn the house down?"

It wasn't often that I had the rapt attention of two adults. Both women stared at me with their cigarettes stuck to their bottom lips.

"What makes you say that, Mary Katherine?" Twig stammered.

"Don't call me that, *Vernice*," I replied. Traffic on Hammond Street was all I could hear for what seemed like forever. I fingered the plastic cowboy's pistol thoughtfully, until finally I was ready to speak, still savoring my rare moment of control.

"I have ears and I have eyes, ladies," was all I said.

"Well, I don't know what trashy talk you've been hearing, but your Uncle Tim was mistakenly accused of setting a fire long ago. He didn't do it and the jury said so and that's the end of it," Twig said.

Nana cleared her throat, but said nothing.

"I believe it's called 'arson for hire'." I dropped the phrase like a duchess letting a silk hanky slip from her fingers.

"Where the hell did you pick up that lingo?" Twig demanded.

A snort escaped from my grandmother.

"She has ears and she has eyes, Vernice," she laughed.

Twig, however, was not laughing.

"The man is no arsonist, Lady Jane," my mother said. Her voice was heavy with threat and the message was clear: shut up. *Now.*

Fat chance. I had the floor, and I wasn't giving it up, not even with the penalty of a smack in the kisser looming.

"Uncle Tim was hired – *accused* of being hired, excuse me – to burn down the campaign headquarters of a candidate for mayor," I said. Neither woman spoke.

"It was in *all* the papers." The feeling of triumph was almost too much to contain. I wanted this moment to last a lifetime. It didn't.

"Bring that up in front of him and you'll be the one burning. Your little ass will be scorched, by God," Twig warned.

"I thought he was *inn-o-cent*, Vernice," I said in a sing-song voice guaranteed to earn me a cuff.

"Watch yourself, little girl," my mother growled. Nana ground her cigarette into the center of one of the crystal ashtrays she'd "borrowed" from Henri's, her chalky lipstick still visible on the end where a filter should be.

"She might say the same to *you*, Vernice."

I wasn't about to be stopped by the likes of Twig. Her threats were empty; she might yank me by the hair occasionally, or give me a good pinch on the underside of my arm, but I could live with those punishments. I was determined to dig around until I got to the bottom of the mystery that was Uncle Tim.

The Favor

There were places in our neighborhood where kids were not welcome. We knew not to go into certain businesses that dotted the main streets, and we knew where unsavory people hung their hats. The "lamp store" was off-limits.

No one ever bought a light fixture from the man named Chicky. His merchandise was coated with decades of dust, and his window displays never changed. The price tags were faded from the sun of twenty summers, and the sign on the door was flipped permanently to read "CLOSED" even though the front door was always open. Men with cigars wedged between their teeth walked in and out of Chicky's Light Emporium, sometimes with paper bags in their hands, sometimes without. Sometimes, they came out tucking white envelopes into their suit coat pockets; other times, they patted their breast pockets, once, twice, three times before driving away in their cars. It was a fascinating place, alright, one worthy of my attention, so you can imagine how excited I was when Uncle Tim asked me to run down to Chicky's as a favor.

Twig would kill me, I knew, but I couldn't care less. She was at the doctor's with little Fitzy, trying to get to the root of his constant wailing. Arlene was obsessing over a Maxwell House coffee can full of buttons, sorting them by size and color. I'd already made the mistake of examining a large brass button with an anchor on it, and this disruption was enough to send Arlene screaming like she'd been stabbed with a kitchen knife.

"Molly, how would you like to earn 50 cents?" Uncle Tim asked.

"Are you kidding? What do I have to do?" I was saving my allowances so that I might one day have my ears pierced. It was a goal I kept to myself, however. Twig was opposed to the idea.

"Where are we? Africa?" she asked when I mentioned my desire to wear hoop earrings.

"What's next? A dish in your lip?" I swear, Twig could be so mean sometimes.

"I need you to go to Chicky's and drop off a package for me," Uncle Tim told me.

"A lamp?" I asked.

"No, just a package, nothin' heavy. Could you?"

"Sure," I said, "Only don't let Twig know. She'd kill me for going near there."

"Our secret," Tim said with a smile. A conspiracy! I was thrilled.

"I'll take Arlene with me," I offered. I knew this would put me in good favor with Uncle Tim.

"Arlene! Ride?" I asked the little girl hovering over her pile of buttons. I took her chin into my hand to make her look at me, but she twisted her face away. Not even the rhythm of the stroller would entice her enough to forget the job she'd set out to do, whatever that was. Sometimes, I'd sit and watch her as closely as I could, trying to figure out how her mind worked, what the purpose of her play might be. It was a mystery bigger than the pyramids, I tell you.

"It's OK, Molly. You can leave her with me. She's no trouble," Uncle Tim told me.

Uncle Tim handed me a used brown paper lunch bag with a grease stain on its bottom. It was double-wrapped at the neck with black electrical tape.

"Bring these…documents… down to Chicky for me. And don't for a minute let your grip go on that bag."

I nodded. He held out three quarters, instead of two.

"And get yourself a little somethin' on the way back," he said.

I nodded again. Pierced earring money *and* a Sky Bar! Nirvana. This errand-running could pay off. I held the bag firmly in my fist. It took everything I had to not open it up and peek inside, but I didn't succumb to the urge. Somehow I knew that tampering with this delivery wasn't a wise idea.

Just a block from Chicky's Light Emporium, Deborah Rice was walking her dog, Patches. Patches was a sweet old thing, with a missing eye and a mangled ear, the result of a long-ago tussle with the meanest cat in the neighborhood, Tuffy Hackett.

"Aptly named," Twig had said, upon seeing what Tuffy had done to Patches.

"Where you headed?" Deborah asked me, eyeing the bag I clutched.

"Just running an errand for my Uncle," I answered casually, but her staring at that bag made me nervous.

"You mean 'Uncle Fire-Starter'? That Uncle?" She smiled.

"He's no firebug," I shot back. "He was acquitted. Why don't you go look that up if you don't know the meaning, huh?"

"That's not what my Dad says. He says your uncle is an *arsonist*. Look THAT up, Miss Fink."

"I don't have to. I know what it means. I also know gossip when I hear it. Now if you'll excuse me, I have an errand to run."

That's when she stepped in front of me like she wasn't going to let me pass.

I knew right then we'd never be friends again. There was something in her look that told me so. Even old Patches growled.

"What's in the bag?" she asked.

"Don't know. Not my business," I replied.

"Let's have a look," she said, making a snatch for it.

"I wouldn't," I warned, and something in the way I said it must've surprised my ex-friend. She stopped lunging.

"Fine. Be a fink," she said with a smile. From the direction of the old garage, I heard a whistle.

"That's my boyfriend Bernie calling me. I've got better things to do than to play silly games with you," Deborah said, and off she went to answer the call, dragging poor old Patches behind. I could only imagine what she and Bernie might be doing while I was buying a Sky Bar.

This notion freed me up to recall once again the Sparhawk penis, which, if I recalled, was substantially larger than baby Fitzy's, the only other penis I'd laid eyes on. I tried to push that unholy thought from my brain as I walked toward Chicky's Light Emporium. The verboten vision lasted only a moment, erased quickly by the reality of my mission: to enter the dark and forbidden world of Uncle Tim. As always, the door was open despite the CLOSED sign. From the street I could smell cigar smoke, and hear music coming from a tinny radio within.

I peered inside just as the Mills Brothers broke into *Those Lazy, Hazy, Crazy Days of Summer,* a WTAG staple. I'd heard my mother sing to it while ironing, and I knew some of the words. No one was singing along at Chicky's.

"Who's the kid?" I heard a man ask from a corner of the display room. I guess that's what you'd call the place where I was standing. All around me were floor lamps and chandeliers, some connected by cobwebs. The protective cellophane sleeves that covered the lampshades were faded to yellow. I was reminded of that terrifying movie I sneaked in to see at the Plymouth – *What Ever Happened to Baby Jane?* I half-expected to see Bette Davis come from behind a door, all baloney curls, red lips and bows. For a place full of light fixtures there was very little light to be had.

From a room I could not see, came a man I did not know. His hair was white-white with no dirty yellow tint like Uncle Roland's, no gray pepper like Nana's.

His skin was more brown than it was white, though not brown-black like a Negro, but more like the color of the caramel in a Bull's Eye. He wore a suit with stripes in it, and a shirt whiter than his white hair. His tie was a print I'd once heard Aunt Annie call "paisley," and in his breast pocket was a handkerchief even whiter than his too-white hair. Whiter still than his handkerchief were his teeth, which he showed by smiling broadly at me.

"Hello, sweetheart," he said, "I think you made a wrong turn on your way to the candy store."

I swallowed hard. "No sir," I began, "I don't think so. My Uncle Tim sent me."

"Medavoy?" he asked sharply.

"Yes, sir."

"It's about time," he said, and with that, he grabbed from my hand the paper bag filled with "documents." With his free hand he fished around in his trouser pocket and came up with a fifty-cent piece with John F. Kennedy's head on it.

"Scram," was all he said as he put the coin in my sweaty hand.

And that's just what I did.

I had a hot pocketful of loot tempting me as I walked past Elmer & Bill's, but I kept on walking, my head too full of questions to spend any of it. Once again, I had no clue what I'd just seen, but it certainly was fascinating.

Uncle Tim was standing on the front porch smoking a cigar with a plastic white tip on it. It made him look elegant, that cigar.

"How'd it go?" he asked casually. Arlene was squatting on the bottom stair, still fussing over her can of buttons. It made me think of what Twig said once about not wasting her money on real toys for the child: "Arlene has her own idea of fun, and it's different from yours and mine."

"Okay, I guess. A guy with a snazzy suit and white hair took the package from me. Is that Chicky?" I asked Uncle Tim.

"Hmm? Yeah, that's him. He say anything to you?"

"Yeah. Scram!"

Uncle Tim chuckled softly. I watched as he pulled a button from his pocket and handed it to Arlene. It was the first time I'd ever seen the child show real gratitude. She grabbed his hand and kissed it.

"Whoa Nelly," I heard myself say.

Round Peg, Square Hole

The whole idea of junior high sickened me. The seventh grade hung over my head like a stink bomb, and as fall neared, I experienced sheer panic. Along with my own dread, Arlene would be entering kindergarten, a thought that worried me to death. What would other children make of her? What would a teacher do with her? Worse yet, what would a teacher do *to* her?

I'd seen how teachers could be around kids who were odd. The paste-eaters, the nose-pickers, the birdbrains. They hated them; you could feel it. They stuck them in the back seat in the last row, near the window, and ignored them as best they could. When they acted up, they were sent out into the hall, to sit in a desk by the cloak room. It was solitary confinement, and I couldn't bear the thought of my sister being exiled from the classroom.

Yet, I knew it would be so. I knew that the first time she was told to sit and didn't, the first time she didn't answer a teacher's question, the first time she shrieked like she'd been zapped with a ray-gun because somebody touched her blocks – which would be lined up according to some bizarre system only Arlene could understand – it would mean banishment to the hallway for sure.

But I was wrong. It never came to that, because the principal sat down with Twig to break it to her that Arlene's quirkiness was a lot more than eccentricity.

"She's retarded," was what the principal of Hammond Street Elementary School told Twig. Mr. Gleason must've been feeling the heat that day. Beneath a window, Arlene balanced on her haunches, thoroughly absorbed in the Maxwell house coffee can I remembered to bring along. I sat holding a fussy Fitzy in my arms while Twig gave the principal the kind of look she usually saved for Aunt Madeline and Uncle Roland: a look of pure disgust.

"Like hell she is," my mother said.

"Excuse me?" Principal Gleason replied.

"You heard me. My child is not retarded. I know retarded when I see it. She's simply marching to a different drummer."

"Mrs. Medavoy, I have here the results of testing done by your pediatrician's office, and I'm afraid that it proves conclusively that your daughter is ... that your daughter's IQ is...substantially lower than average."

"Define 'average,' if you would," Twig dared him.

"Mrs. Medavoy, I'm not here to argue. I'm here to help you. We would do that child no good service by enrolling her here. She needs specialized assistance. Perhaps with proper training she'll someday be...a productive member of society. Employable."

The sweat was rolling off Gleason's forehead now like the windows at the coin-op Laundromat.

"Employable. *Employable*," Twig repeated.

"Employable. Employable," Arlene echoed.

This was taking a very bad turn, I could see it. I braced myself for the inevitable, but this time, she tricked me.

Instead of blasting away at Gleason, she simply gathered up from his desk the papers that read "Medavoy, Arlene V." She stuffed them into Fitzy's diaper bag and headed for the door. I scrambled to my feet, nearly dropping Fitzy in the process. Arlene followed, her button can clutched to her chest.

"Mrs. Medavoy? Mrs. Medavoy. I have here a list of ...schools..." was what I heard Gleason saying as I carried my brother through the gleaming ready-for-first-day corridor. Outside, Twig was attempting to light an L&M against the wind.

"Twig," I began, as I slipped a wailing Fitzy into the pram, "Mr. Gleason was trying to tell you about some schools for Arlene."

"Schools? *Schools*? Let me tell you about those schools," Twig said, her eyes wet with tears. Rarely did I see her cry; Frank's death only wet her eyes, but not since JFK's head was shot full of holes had I seen her this way.

"Those aren't schools he's suggesting, Molly. He's talking about institutions, hellholes, where they keep people they don't understand out of sight."

I'd recently seen *The Miracle Worker* with Patty Duke as Helen Keller, which had me pretending to be sightless for a few days. Now I had visions of Arlene being sent to the Tewkesbury Home for the Blind, where Annie Sullivan and her tubercular brother Jimmy went as kids. Jimmy died there, I recalled, while Annie's eyes nearly rotted out of her head from neglect.

"Whoa, that's no good," I said.

"No good, no good, no good," Arlene agreed.

"I'll be damned if I'll stick her in some convenient place, out of sight, out of mind. Forgotten," Twig said, words meant to be bold and brave, spoken in a wobbly voice.

My heart broke a little for Twig right then. It broke for all of us.

———◇———

Fall came. So did junior high.

The bus ride was a nightmare, from the get-go. Deborah Rice had ceased acknowledging me as human. I sat alone.

At Hammond Street Elementary sixth graders were top bananas. At Woodbury Junior High, seventh graders were lepers. Eighth graders tripped us, lobbed spitballs at us and generally treated us like something smelly they stepped in. Ninth graders so despised us that we were simply invisible, not worthy of torture. I'd rather ride a ninth-grade bus any day, since I could slip on and off unnoticed. On the other buses, I was told I possessed "a pirate's dream" - a sunken chest.

I buried my nose in books during those horrid trips. I'd graduated to anything written by Charles Dickens, and as I entered the seventh grade, I was deeply involved in the lives of Oliver Twist and Fagin. I was tempted to ask the sweaty cafeteria lady with the hairnet and the arms made of pudding for "more fish heads and gravy," but I stopped myself. I was truly alone in my desire to read every book ever written, and even more alone in my determination to one day be a writer.

It was a rainy day in October when the school nurse herded my homeroom into the hallway outside her office.

"Eye exam," I heard Deborah Rice say to her new best friend, Patricia Landry. They were wearing friendship rings to prove it. This news caused me no small worry, since I'd recently noticed that the chalkboard was a bit blurry from where I sat.

"E. M? Z? 3… that might be an N," I stumbled.

"I see glasses in your future," the nurse told me.

My greatest fear realized: adding insult to injury by slapping glasses on this already ignored specimen. "Just kill me," was my first thought. My second thought was to runaway, hobo-style, carrying a bindle stick and riding the rails ala Steinbeck. I felt about as popular as Lennie Small already; I might as well carry dead mice in my pockets if I was going to wear glasses.

Twig wasn't thrilled by the idea, either, but only because she couldn't squeak the extra cash out of the budget. That's when Uncle Tim stepped in, knocking the wind right out of Twig.

Quietly, over a cup of my mother's muddy coffee, he said, "Twig, if the kid needs glasses, she's getting glasses."

And that was that. Next thing I knew I was sitting in front of a mirror in the showroom of

Community Eyewear, trying to find frames that didn't make me look like a fink.

"Those are beautiful! You look like a movie star!" The optician crowed. There were only six styles to pick from in frames made to fit the world's tiniest skull. I had on the least offensive pair I could find in the lot; I only hoped they'd draw attention away from the growing-out permanent wave that framed my face.

"I look like an asshole," I murmured, swiftly followed by "Ow!" as Twig snatched up a lock of hair and pulled mightily.

It was determined by the eye doctor that I only needed the glasses for reading. That meant I could whip them off my face when I looked up from whatever work was in front of me during school. That also meant carrying them back and forth from home to school, from school to home. It only took a week before I managed to crush them between my US History book, *Great Expectations* and my three-ring binder.

"Nice," my mother said, when I took them out of the flimsy fabric eyeglass case with the groovy paisley print that I'd insisted on having before leaving Community Eyewear. The lenses sparkled like new-fallen snow on the kitchen table, tumbling and tinkling from the sleeve when I pulled out the frames.

Part of me was thrilled. Part of me was sad. Though I'd rather die than admit it to Twig, I could read for hours without headaches since getting those glasses.

"Do you need these to see the chalkboard in class?" The optician asked me as he fitted me anew. Stupidly, I replied: "Yes."

I was now a full-time glasses-wearing fink during every waking moment, and sometimes more than that, should I fall asleep reading, which I did every night of my wretched life. If they were real and alive and standing in front of me, I bet even Lennie Small and Boo Radley wouldn't take me to the Christmas dance I read about on the flier outside my homeroom while wearing my new glasses.

Crying Uncle

There was no sympathy coming from my mother when it came to my wearing glasses. Twig said I'd ruined my eyes reading at night with a flashlight under the covers to keep from waking everybody else who slept in our room. It was a crowded place, for certain, and I didn't want to wake either Fitzy or Arlene with a blazing bedside lamp, so I read my books with the bedspread pulled over my head. I wasn't giving up reading along with room to breathe.

I didn't bother to tell my mother my eyes had been ruined long before the flashlight got them. Now that I had glasses, I realized I hadn't been able to see for a very long time. I was loath to admit this, of course, and I still grumbled like a troll when I put them on my face each morning, but I was secretly grateful for them. It was infinitely better to be able to see than to go through life squinting at shapes and guessing.

I decided it was also better to be able to see than to attract a boy. I finally came to the conclusion that I'd be either a nun or a reclusive writer who contacts her publisher from a mountain aerie. The choice wasn't very difficult since religion wasn't high on my list and the idea of wearing those stiff bibs didn't do much for me. On the plus side, that nun's headgear meant no bobby pins, bangs or permanents, and that appealed to me. But living a life so pure that Confession was a breeze was not in the cards for me. I opted for the role of brilliant recluse.

By now, I'd discovered plays. After watching Marlon Brando go toe-to-toe with Vivian Leigh, I decided to investigate Mr. Tennessee Williams. I was mesmerized. Stage direction became an obsession with me – I began thinking out everyday routines as if they were designed for the theater. People entered rooms from stage left; the curtain rose and fell on meals and discussions. The living room furniture became props. Uncle Tim became a *protagonist.*

All this reading kept me from thinking about my real aggravation: the Christmas dance, to be held in two days. I knew I wasn't going to be asked by any boy to actually attend this event. Girls in Miss

Lee's homeroom were talking about the dresses they'd seen at Barnard's and Denholm's, or the dresses they'd already bought at Eddy's. I buried my face in *Night of the Iguana*. That is, until my homeroom teacher caught a glimpse of the title of the book I was hiding behind.

"What are you reading?" Miss Lee asked. I told her. Wasn't it obvious, I thought, by the print on the cover?

"That is entirely inappropriate reading material for a young lady," she said, and snatched the book from my hands.

"Hey! That's a library book! I have to return it tomorrow!" I exclaimed, and the Christmas dance chatter went dead. All eyes were on me.

"Why the librarian would allow you to check out such ...*material*..." she trailed off in disgust.

"What's wrong with it?" I asked, and not in my most polite voice. I was barking right back at her, and I knew I should be putting a lid on it, but I was too angry to care.

Miss Lee spun around dervish-like, her eyes narrowed into little slits.

"Your tone, Mary Katherine, will change, do you hear me?"

"Give me back my book and then it will change," I heard myself say.

"Whoa!" The class let out a collective murmur. Stand-offs with Miss Lee were unheard of, and here I was committing suicide over *a book,* of all things.

The bench outside Mr. Cipro's office was a cold one. It was worn in the middle like an old saddle from holding the sorry butts of idiots like me.

We were looking each other in the eye, Mr. Cipro and me, like two cats fighting for turf. There was no way I was leaving his office without that book in my hand. Old Man Cipro was no push-over, either. This was a battle of the Titans.

"Young lady, I don't believe we've ever met before," he began. This, of course, was true, because I wasn't the sort of student who regularly wound up on his bench. I didn't break the rules. I didn't cause a commotion in the lunch hall. I was never tardy. My skirts weren't too short and my phone number wasn't etched on the boys' room wall for a good time.

"No sir," I mumbled. "I'm a good kid."

"Well, quite often good kids come in here to show me their good work."

I said nothing. I'd never been told by a teacher to bring my work to the front office for Show and Tell. I'd earned many an "A" on my papers and never once was I put on parade. This made me suspect he was full of malarkey.

"Yes, well," he ahem-ed. "Miss Lee tells me you're reading…inappropriate material in her classroom."

"No sir."

"Miss Lee is mistaken? Is that what you're saying?"

"No," I said, "Miss Lee is just plain wrong."

"Really? Well, Miss Lee has been teaching Home Economics here for 23 years. I think she knows inappropriate material when she sees it." He leaned in on "23" and I caught a whiff of Aqua Velva.

"No, she doesn't," I said. "She teaches cooking and sewing. Not English."

"According to Miss Lee, this play you're reading discusses adult subject matter well beyond your years."

"How would she know that? The last book I read was *Death in Venice* by Thomas Mann." I made sure I pronounced "Mann" the right way – Mahhhn – to prove I was no fool.

"And before that I read *L' Enfants Terrible* by Jean Cocteau," I added. "If Miss Lee wants to talk material with me, I'll discuss corduroy, but not books."

It didn't take long for Mr. Cipro to dial SW9-6714.

"Mrs. Medavoy? This is Mr. Cipro, vice-principal of Woodbury Junior High. I have your daughter Mary Katherine sitting here in my office…no, she hasn't been hurt. No… she's not ill. What she is, Mrs. Medavoy is suspended, for three days from school, for belligerence and for having in her possession inappropriate material."

Twig couldn't come to the school to cart my insolent arse home. Fitzy was sick again, and Nana wasn't answering her phone, either. Since it had to be a family member who could collect me, Uncle Tim was assigned the task. It was his face I saw peeking around the thick opaque glass door of Mr. Cipro's office.

After listening to Mr. Cipro's version of our conversation, Uncle Tim sat for a moment. Finally, he turned and asked me if what the vice-principal said seemed accurate to me. I said that it was a true account, but double-checking the word of an adult with a kid was enough to send Old Man Cipro into conniptions.

"See here, Medavoy," he blustered, but Uncle Tim waved him off.

"Mr. Cipro," he started, "Have you read this play?"

"No sir, I have not. But the word of a faculty member is enough for me."

Tim looked at me again.

"Molly, what might your teacher object to in this book?"

"Alcoholism, maybe. Or a man leaving the priesthood because he has sexual urges."

"My Lord! Of course that's inappropriate!" Mr. Cipro interrupted.

"Molly, were either of those subjects new or strange to you? Were you confused by them?" Tim asked.

"Of course not," I said. "Uncle Roland is a drunk, and nobody with brains stands too close to Father Vail."

And that is how Uncle Tim got the book back and I got out of the Christmas dance: suspension from school meant no participation in extracurricular activities.

"What dance? You never mentioned it," Uncle Tim said, as we walked home from school four hours earlier than the rest of the kids. We'd stopped for a soda before facing Twig, and I was still chewing on the straw.

"Oh, just a dance," I muttered. "I wasn't going anyway."

"Why not?"

"Well, because I don't know how to dance, for one thing, and for another, no one asked me."

"Dopes and donkeys," was all my uncle had to say about that.

Despite my own miserable existence, the world around me continued to spin. Uncle Tim was heartbroken over the announcement that Sandy Koufax was retiring because of arthritis.

"Man, what a sin," he moaned over the sports page. "The Dodgers were payin' him 125 grand a year. A *year*. Think about it, Molly."

"What would you do with all that money, Uncle?" I asked when I looked up from Brenda Starr.

"Plenty, little girl, plenty," he said.

"Well, I know what I would do," I began. "I'd move us into a bigger house and find a doctor or a teacher who could make Arlene talk like a regular kid and make Twig and Fitzy happier."

"Nothing for yourself?"

"Those things would be for myself, trust me," I said.

Uncle Tim let out a little snort-laugh and went back to the sports page. We'd begun a ritual, my uncle and me, without ever speaking of it; we read the paper together every evening. He'd comment on various tragedies and triumphs while I'd keep him abreast of the comic world. Most nights, we'd do the "Jumbles" together. We were both good at spotting the word that hid inside the scrambled letters. It was like a race, and if I found the word before he did, he gave me a quarter. I don't doubt that more than once he let me win the 25-cent piece by holding back the answer long enough for me to figure it. It was times like these that made me scratch my head, wondering why anyone ever saw him as "a bad penny," to quote Aunt Annie.

It was a Friday night – fish sticks and green beans – when Uncle Tim came in from having a few at the Third Base Bar (Last stop before home.) He was tipsy, but smiling, so I wasn't afraid of him, like I would be if he were Uncle Roland. Uncle Roland was a nasty drunk, according to Nana.

"You can tell an unhappy person by the way liquor hits," my grandmother deduced.

"If you have a knot in your shorts when you're sober, it doesn't loosen with booze. It gets tighter right along with you."

I had to assume that Uncle Tim's shorts were hanging loose, since he was one happy son-of-a-gun that evening. He lifted a cold fish stick from the broiler pan, brought it to his nose and declared it "DOA" before letting it drop into the waste basket.

"Dead on Arrival, ladies. This is no supper for a bevy of beauties such as yourselves."

"Molly, run down to P&T's and order up – let's see – one, two, three – Arlene can share mine, she won't eat a whole order – three orders of fish and chips with plenty of slaw on the side – don't forget the tartar sauce – and these fish sticks are history, Twig. History!"

He pulled from his pants pocket a wad of cash the likes of which I'd only seen in movies, and, occasionally, the hand of Chicky the lamp proprietor when I dropped off Uncle Tim's brown bag. That secret chore had become a weekly goldmine for me.

Cheerfully pulling from the roll a ten-dollar bill, Uncle Tim slapped it into my outstretched palm hard enough to cause a happy sting to my skin.

"And for your troubles, you, Senorita, may keep the change," he told me.

At two bucks an order, I knew I was in the money. Four bucks? For trotting down to P&T's and ordering up the most delicious fish dinners on the planet Earth? I couldn't find my shoes fast enough.

I was heading out the door when the last thing I heard was Twig's quizzing: "Hit the Trifecta, Tim?" but I didn't hang around long enough to hear the answer, if there was one.

Twig vs. Twiggy

As the daughter of a woman whose middle child was seen as an imbecile and whose baby was thought to be illegitimate, I wasn't invited to many sleepovers. In 1966, these were not considered the makings of an acceptable friend by most parents, though what harm would come to their precious children, I couldn't guess. How a flat-chested four-eyed bookworm would have a negative impact on their lives escaped me.

I survived seventh grade by the skin of my teeth, shunned by most boys – and the girls who beguiled them - because of my deadly case of nerdiness. I had all the appeal of a leper after I won the blue ribbon in the Science Fair and by the time my maps of the seven continents were on display in Mr. Howard's geography class, I was considered social poison. There was no recovering from it, so I decided to embrace it and become a nuclear physicist. Or a brain surgeon. Or the Supreme Winner of All Spelling Bees. I wanted to get the highest grade, have the best project, write the finest essays, because, well, once I realized that being brainy was my destiny no matter how unfair, I vowed to be the best leper, the best nerd, the best dweeb of them all. I held fast to the idea that books made better friends than humans, especially the sub-humans who made up most of my classes.

Word got around that I my IQ was off the charts, which wasn't true. I was simply smarter because I read a lot and retained stuff – and when teachers taught, I listened. I realized early on that teachers weren't rocket scientists necessarily; they just had diplomas that gave them permission to mold me into what they considered to be an Upstanding Contributor to Society. My guidance counselor, Mr. Dumas, called me in to his office one day toward the end of the school year and asked me if I would like to skip the eighth grade.

"Your teachers feel that you will be bored in eighth grade, Molly," Mr. Dumas told me. "They feel that you have the foundation academically and the emotional maturity to enter ninth grade in the fall."

I chewed on this for a while. There was nothing to keep me in the same grade with the same kids who were creeps to me, and I was bored, alright. Maybe this would bring about The

Transformation. I'd accepted myself as ugly duckling-like, while waiting to miraculously turn into that swan I'd heard so much about. Maybe older kids would see my worth and have similar interests. Maybe.

"Of course, you will need to talk it over with your parents," he added.

"Parent," I said. "My father is dead."

"Oh. I'm sorry. I didn't know. It's not in your transcripts. Did he pass away recently?"

I thought this over. Frank was gone long before he "passed away," long before his ill-fated escape to the great state of Texas.

"Long ago. I never knew him," was all I said.

Once home, I didn't bring up the subject just yet. I had to think about this, and I knew that Twig would be of little help in my decision-making. She had a way of clouding the issue at hand.

Twig decided the Beatles were a bad influence after John Lennon put his foot in his mouth by saying the Fab Four were more popular than Jesus. This led to her confiscating my collection of 45s, sifting through it for "trash." My records were purchased with the cash I earned running paper sacks for Uncle Tim; for 85 cents, I could buy anything I heard on WORC, the local top-40 radio station. For Christmas, Uncle Tim gave me a transistor radio with earplugs, and all I had to do when I wanted to tune out Twig, Arlene and Fitzy was tune into Jeff Starr, the handsome disc jockey who played the hits. When I heard a song I really liked, I could buy it and play it on the rinky-dink record player that skipped unless I put a quarter on the arm.

"Those boys started out wholesome, but something has happened to them along the way," Twig grumbled as she riffled through my 45s. "I never did like that John. He had a smart-alecky way from Day One."

I hadn't seen it, but word was the Beatles had made an album with a strange cover that sent parents and preachers into orbit. They were posed with hacked-up baby dolls and butchered meat, I heard, but no one I knew had a copy. I was itching to see it, thinking anything that caused Twig to fly off the handle had to have some merit. I mentioned this mystery album to Uncle Tim.

"*Yesterday and Today*, I've seen it," he said. I just looked at Tim. I never knew what he knew, but he knew plenty.

When *Paperback Writer* was released, I bought it and hid it between the mattress and the box spring. I wasn't going to let Twig's obsession with all things Beatle stop me from listening. While I was under there, I found two pieces of petrified bologna, which explained the mysterious smell I'd been unable to pinpoint. Apparently, Arlene had discovered a new hiding place.

The "British invasion" was everywhere. Miniskirts had Twig in a tizzy, due to the size of her thighs, and she said so – over and over again, especially since an emaciated blonde with enormous eyes named "Twiggy" was on every magazine cover.

"Pick a dress off a rack at Zayre's and it looks like they forgot to finish it," she moaned. "I held one up to me in the mirror and I swear to God it only came to my hips. There's not enough material there to cover your privates!"

The mod fashions coming out of England fascinated me, but my fascination turned to horror when my mother decided her weight shouldn't stop her from keeping up with the style trends. She found a psychedelic-print dress that fell mid-thigh and accessorized herself with a pair of earrings that looked like fuzzy marbles. All of this I could handle until she pulled from a Morse Shoe bag a pair of white go-go boots. They hugged her calves like Saran Wrap, which is not the way they fit the legs of models in the pages of Glamour magazine.

"What do you think, Mol?"

She was standing in the bedroom with the tags still dangling from her sleeve. The patent leather go-go-boots strained against her fleshy calves. Before I could answer, Nana came in from hanging wash rags on the clothesline out back.

"Halloween come early this year, Vernice?" she asked with a grin.

I saw Twig's face fall from hopeful to broken. Without a word she wriggled out of the dress, yanked the earrings from her lobes and tugged mightily at the go-go boots until they popped free. Wearing only her Playtex girdle and bra, she stuffed it all in a Zayre's bag.

"What did I say?" Nana turned to me for an explanation. Twig headed to the bathroom and slammed the door.

"Nana, I love you a lot, but sometimes you aren't very nice to my mother," I said.

Never in my life had I ever spoken this way to my Nana, and never in my life had I taken Twig's side over my grandmother.

"Well, somebody had to say it," she sniffed, and with that, she headed home.

"She gone?" Twig poked her head out of the bathroom.

"Yup. Hey, Twig?"

No answer.

"I thought you looked very pretty."

No answer.

"Mom," I added, awkwardly.

Twig blinked through tears and walked away, and from that moment on, I never again called her Vernice.

Molly vs. the World

So began my Summer of Fear: all over the news were stories of horror that caused me to lie awake at night. Thanks to a pock-marked loser named Richard Benjamin Speck, I could not sleep without checking the locks on the windows twice before climbing into bed with the covers pulled tight over my head. After he slaughtered eight nurses in their dorm, I was certain it was our fate. Twig said she could swing a bat faster than any man could jab a knife, but I wasn't comforted by her bravado. When it was discovered that a ninth nurse escaped Speck's knife by hiding under a bed, I began sleeping underneath the double bed I still shared with Twig. (By now, Arlene was sleeping wherever she pleased, and often enough we found her curled at the foot of the bed like a puppy, or on a scatter rug. She was bothered by our touch, and no longer could tolerate sleeping with us.) For me, the threat of the slats giving way under the weight of Twig and inevitable suffocation by box spring was a small price to pay for a sliver of comfort.

"Are you ever going to sleep up here again?" Twig asked, her head hanging over the side of the bed. Her hair swept the floor as she peered underneath where I had constructed a snug hideout.

"Not likely," I answered before checking to make sure the kitchen knife I had taped to a bed slat was still there.

That was July of 1966. My terror was compounded when in August a former Marine named Charles Whitman climbed up into the University of Texas clock tower and massacred 16 people as they strolled the campus. He picked them off one by one, and injured 32 more before police were able to shoot him dead.

"Texas again," Twig wondered aloud. I was thinking the same thing, especially after news reports revealed that Richard Speck had spent a good deal of his miserable life in Dallas.

"You couldn't get me to visit that state for a million bucks," Aunt Annie said. While they sipped cold beer, I crawled under my bed and ran a finger over the serrated edge of the kitchen knife.

Every tall building I passed suddenly held the potential to provide a maniac with a perch. The City Hall clock tower would forever be a downtown location I shunned, and I began to bite my fingernails.

Adding to my terror were the blurry photos on the cover of *The National Enquirer*, the tabloid that stared up at me from the magazine racks at Elmer and Bill's. Long before these massacres, Nana had warned me about that newspaper.

When I asked her if she ever read it, she replied:

"I don't own a bird to line the cage, and I don't go fishing to wrap the guts. So, no need for it."

That newspaper. It haunted me. Images of children crushed under the tires of trucks, Speck's hideous face sneering up from the front page: I was repelled and drawn to the headlines at the same time. How could this be?

At home, Twig didn't consider my fears drastic enough to explore them. Only Uncle Tim asked why my nails were chewed down to a bloody mess.

"I'm a little nervous about school. I'm skipping 8th grade, you know."

I'd finally gotten around to admitting I'd had enough of the same kids whose once-dirty faces now sported pimples. I'd been surrounded by the same classmates since I was in kindergarten and frankly, I couldn't take another year of them. I'd long ago stopped knocking on Deborah's door; she buddied around with girls who filled their bras with their own flesh and smoked Kents. Older kids HAD to be better than these jamokes.

"I know. That's not what's buggin' you, is it? I mean, school's a breeze for you. What's really eatin' at you?"

I paused before answering. I suddenly felt like a big baby, admitting I had conjured up boogie men that scared the bejeezus out of me.

"The world," I whispered. I'd never been so close to tears in front of Uncle Tim. It occurred to me that I never let myself cry in front of anyone.

"Is that all? Just the whole world? I thought it was somethin' BIG," he grinned.

I didn't answer. If he was poking fun at me I would have to hate him forever, and I truly hoped he wasn't going to force that to happen.

Uncle Tim took me by the shoulders. His face was only inches from mine.

"I know you've been sleepin' under your bed. I know you're afraid that no place is safe, and maybe you aren't wrong, Molly. I don't know. The world is a pretty shitty place most of the time. All I can say is this: as long as I'm breathin' no one will cause you harm. Not you, or your sister and brother, or Twig. Got that?"

"But you can't be everywhere," I blubbered, having lost my battle to keep my tears in check.

"You'd be amazed," he said with a smile.

That night, I slept in bed with Twig. I was pretty sure she was wishing I stayed "down under" by the third time I elbowed her ribs for snoring, but if she did, she never said so.

No Place Like Home

There seemed to be no place for Arlene; after Twig's clash with the principal regarding my sister's "condition," the subject of schooling her was dropped. I'm sure Twig knew she couldn't go on forever without some kind of education, but her attentions were focused on Fitzy, who had more health problems than the pediatric ward at St. Vincent Hospital might see in a week. Everything he ate caused rashes to appear on his pale skin, and his stomach was never happy, either. If he wasn't constipated and crying from the cramps, he was crying over gas pains and loaded diapers. He slept fitfully and never smiled. The boy was a puzzle - as if Arlene wasn't mystery enough for one family.

The person most intolerant of Fitzy's endless wailing was Arlene. Whenever he started crying, she covered her ears and ran in circles with her eyes squeezed shut, until she bumped blindly into a piece of furniture or a door jamb. The vacuum cleaner had a similar effect on her, as did the tea kettle's whistle, sirens, and the voice of Olive Oyl. Oddly enough, the child wasn't bothered by things that scare most kids. She was completely mesmerized by thunder and lightning. Darkness never seemed to bother her, but Olive Oyl sent her shrieking. Go figure.

Uncle Tim remained Arlene's favorite human being. She made no eye contact with him, but when he came through the door, she raced to meet him, taking him by the hand to see what particular oddity had her attention. It was a rare thing for her to grab the hand of another person, and rarer still for her to care if anyone else should be interested in what pleased or intrigued her. No such bond existed between Arlene and Twig, nor was there any meaningful connection between myself and my sister.

The bond between my uncle and Arlene only strengthened after the kitten arrived.

Uncle Tim's jacket bulged and squirmed on a day when it was clearly too hot to wear a jacket at all. When he unzipped it to reveal the source of the squirm, a mewing fuzzball jumped from the warmth of his midsection. Arlene's Chicklet-tooth smile was the widest I'd ever seen.

"Just what I need: another mouth to feed," Twig harrumphed.

"No worries, Twig. I'll buy the food for it. A stray we fed at work had a litter of five and the momma was run over by the roach coach. Bunch of us decided to each take one baby home."

Twig looked at Tim with an eyebrow arched.

"And besides," Tim continued, "I thought maybe it would help Arlene, maybe draw her out a little."

Twig had no weapons left in her arsenal.

I guess you could call what Uncle Tim was doing with Arlene "home-schooling." I don't recall words to describe it back then, and perhaps there were plenty of families making that choice, but Uncle Tim seemed like Annie Sullivan, Helen Keller's miracle-working teacher, for all he was trying to do with my sister.

"She likes order," he told us one morning, as my mother squawked about finding Arlene's latest collection of contraband.

"Cereal?? Under my coffee table?" Twig cried.

"It's not cereal, at least not to Arlene. It's a puzzle, solved. Look."

He wasn't wrong. When I looked at it again – maybe this time with eyes not so quick to judge – I saw a pattern: the flakes were placed evenly with the raisins, all along a straight line. Three flakes, two raisins.

I looked at the braided rug that covered most of our living room floor, the one Twig had braided and sewn together from scraps of felt she'd been given by our neighbor Mr. Wittner, who worked the 3 to 11 shift at the Millbury Fabric and Dye Company. The same pattern of beige and reddish-brown that made up the rug was found in her cereal puzzle.

Tim knew instinctively what we couldn't see. He saw what Arlene saw, and I wished I had their vision. There was something between them that I was not privy to, nor would I ever be, and as far away from understanding them as I was, Twig was a mile behind me.

"All I see is a mess to be swept," Twig said after surveying the evidence. "None of which tells me she knows her ABCs or ever will."

The ABCs were the least of our problems. The kitten was a tool, I would discover – much later than I might have realized as an adult. In 1966, or any other year, Arlene cared about two things in her world – Uncle Tim and the kitten he gave her.

"Twig. Why do you talk in front of her like she's invisible? Or deaf?"

I saw in Twig's eyes tears that she worked hard to contain. It took a moment for the words to come. She was looking at the cereal – raisin – cereal train that my sister had created and was still perfecting.

"She's not invisible." Twig's voice became so small I could barely hear it without leaning in, though the idea of moving an inch was not on the table.

"I am," she whispered. "I'm the invisible mother. This child doesn't know I'm alive."

Arlene turned to Uncle Tim, and the kitten that slept in his lap. She placed her own head beside the cat's, and guided my uncle's hand to smooth the pet's fur. Twig left the room.

So much would happen before I would have a glimpse into the place where Tim's heart met Arlene's.

Ashes to Ashes

The smell hit my nose first, long before I saw the smoke or the flames. I heard the sirens, but sirens were a regular thing on Chestnut Street, with two hospitals bookending the two-mile stretch, and so I thought nothing of it. I'd taken the #30 bus to downtown that day, where I spent hours in the city library with that same nose buried in "The Grapes of Wrath," and after buying a hot dog at Coney Island, I realized I didn't have enough money for the bus ride home. I had plenty of cash stashed at home, but I didn't like to take much with me when I traveled. Because of my growling belly, I had to walk home. It was a cloudless Saturday afternoon in late April, I recall, when tree buds take on that impossible shade of lime green that they lose upon opening.

That smell. As I got closer, shifting my library books from hip to hip, the acrid stench couldn't be ignored. The snarled traffic, the fire engines, the ambulance – all of it – came into focus as I picked up my pace. I could feel my heart quicken as my legs carried me, until I was running, running, dropping the library books one by one. Those books didn't matter anymore; not when I saw that 204 Chestnut was burning.

Flames were chewing up my home.

I shoved my way through the small crowd of neighbors gathered on the sidewalk, until I found my mother, standing as still as any mannequin in Denholm's window. Beside her stood my grandmother, and just behind her, Uncle Tim, whose pant leg Arlene held in her grubby grip. Plastered against her chest with her other arm was the kitten Uncle had given her.

Twig didn't seem to see or hear me. Her gaze was fixed on the front door.

It wasn't until a firefighter came through it carrying a bundle of rags in his arms that she came to life. The bundle was my brother Fitzy, and before any of these images could tie themselves together for me, Twig was hurried into the ambulance with her dying baby.

That's when I noticed Nana. Her eyes were so narrow I thought they were closed, but she could see, alright. What she stared at was Uncle Tim.

I went to her, touched her arm, shook her a little. She said nothing. She only moved forward when the policeman jerked Uncle Tim's hands behind his back and roughly snapped handcuffs on his wrist. It took both of us to pry Arlene's fingers from his pant leg, as two officers shoved our uncle into the back seat of a cruiser. We were led away from the fire by neighbors.

Aunt Annie poured a shot of whiskey for Nana as we sat at her kitchen table. For me, she made a cup of tea, but my shaking hands couldn't manage to squeeze the bag. Arlene stood by the open window, her grip on the mewing kitten not loosened.

Finally, Nana spoke.

"He confessed. Said he lit the fire himself. Bastard didn't even give a reason. Just said he did it."

I pushed my chair away from the table. That was all I heard before I fainted, just like in the movies. But not like the movies, because instead of landing softly like some countess with a case of the vapors, I fell on my face and busted my glasses.

We lost everything in that fire – my books, my secret stash, my meager wardrobe, which was replaced by the Red Cross. The birds died, of course. Baby pictures, Chatty Cathy, the television, all destroyed in minutes. Our lives were reduced to a pile of trash fit for the Dirty Block, with sopping-wet stuffed animals and a twisted-up bird cage sticking out from insulation and the remains of burnt linoleum. Neighbors were quite kind, though they whispered plenty about our tragedy. Nana housed us until we were placed in a new apartment by the same case workers who brought me new shoes, new underwear, eyeglasses and a mattress that was free of urine stains. In the center of the rubbish pile, nearly obscured by what was once a box spring, stood my mother's safe. Days after the fire trucks left and onlookers forgot about us, I gave the safe's dial a spin. Inside I found a pristine sleeve of Girl Scout Thin Mints. I closed the safe, wiped off the top and sat down. As tears ran down my smudged cheeks, I ate every last one.

The funeral for Fitzy was private. There was no eulogy to say for a baby who never learned to take a step or say a word. His life had been fraught with discomfort, as far as I could tell. Secretly, I wondered if his unfortunate beginning mapped out his sad ending, but there was no one I could approach with that thought. Naming a baby after an assassinated president was always asking for trouble, in my opinion, and I suspect it still.

If Richard Speck had filled my nightmares, he was bumped from the lead by my own flesh and blood. Uncle Tim, with his mask of normalcy, became as terrifying to me as any mass murderer or Hollywood creature. Regularly, he inhabited my dreams, causing me to wake short-winded. On the outside, I appeared to have "adjusted well," according to the social worker's note pad I peeked at while she was freshening up. People see what they want to see, I suppose. I would muddle through four years of high school, but there was little joy to be found there. If my oddball ways as a smarty-pants weren't enough to isolate me, my scandalous family made me social poison, and I set my sights on college. My grades were always top-notch, but my refusal to join clubs and my "clique-less" status made scholarships harder to earn than I'd thought. Finally, I was granted a "full boat" to a small college in New Hampshire. The idea of leaving it all behind kept me going, though the specter of Uncle Tim might have followed me there, until I got the answers I sought from the only person who had them to give.

———◇———

It would be years before I would muster what it took to visit my uncle. The prison where he would spend the rest of his life for setting the fire that killed my brother was not likely to allow a child in to visit without an adult, and no adult would accompany me. When I turned 18, I rode the bus that would bring me to MCI-Cedar Junction.

For many moments I said nothing; all the speeches I'd formulated while riding the bus disintegrated.

Tim was barely recognizable. A few of his teeth were missing, and his nose looked as though it had been reshaped for him more than once by cellmates.

He smoked an entire Marlboro before finally asking me:

"How's it goin'?"

I had to string together a reply.

"I'm starting college in the fall," I mumbled.

"Now, that's swell news," he said. "Scholarship?"

"Huh? Yeah. Scholarship."

"How's Twig?" he asked next. "And...Arlene?"

I had to think about it. Twig was never right after Fitzy died. She finally lost all the weight she wanted to lose, but it was only because food brought her no comfort. Arlene was still Arlene in many ways, but small gains were made in the years following Fitzy's death. My sister was doing pretty well since the fire, I explained, when the department of social services stepped in and realized she was not enrolled in any school.

"Arlene still lives at home. A bus takes her to a special school Monday through Friday. She rolled over on that kitten and smothered it not long after the fire," I reported.

Talk of Arlene made a change come over Uncle Tim. He cleared his throat a few times, moved closer to the mesh screen that separated us.

"You and me, Molly, we've always understood each other, am I right?"

"Before the fire I would have said yes to that," I replied, "But it turns out I didn't know you at all."

My tone stung, I could see. He played with the stubbed-out cigarette in the ashtray before speaking in a voice so low, I could hardly catch his words.

"I mean, we had our secrets, no?"

"We did," I said, "because I trusted you."

"I didn't set that fire."

I needed to hear it again. I thought for sure I was mistaken, but he repeated it.

"If you didn't do it, who did?"

Uncle Tim stared at me hard, as if he were trying to get me to understand without saying the words. That's when I knew.

"Arlene?" I whispered.

"I was napping on the sofa. Your mother asked me to babysit, but I fell asleep. She got ahold of those matches. By the time I realized what she'd done, I couldn't even get to Fitzy's crib. It was all I could do to scoop her up and get out the door."

It made sense. Arlene as arsonist made sense.

"Why didn't you tell that to the police? Why did you confess if you didn't do it?"

Uncle Tim rubbed both eyes with the heels of his palms just as I'd seen Arlene do many times, rubbed them so hard they were raw when he was through.

"One more secret, between us, Molly? Just one? But you have to take it with you all your life. If you don't want to carry it, I'll stop talkin' now. Just say the word."

Odd as it may seem, I knew then that I couldn't leave that terrible place without pledging my loyalty to this strange man, my father's brother.

I nodded.

"I confessed to make things right."

"How?"

"I confessed because I lit that fire back in '56 and got away with it," he whispered.

"I was supposed to burn down an empty buildin' for two grand, but there was a guy inside. I didn't know he was there. But it don't matter that I didn't mean to kill the guy. *I killed the guy*.

"Confessing seemed like a way to keep Arlene safe and make amends. This place," he said, sweeping the air with his hand, "This place is where I belong. Not Arlene.

"Now go away from here, and don't visit me again. This is no place for a pretty young college girl. I'll havta get into a coupla fights tonight just defendin' your honor if any of these sleazebags makes cracks about you."

He smiled, and for a minute I saw my Uncle Tim as he once was, going over the day's news with me in the kitchen.

I had plenty to consider during the long ride home. I thought about how true it was that you never know a person, just as Atticus Finch said. I mulled over a scenario with Arlene institutionalized. I saw her in a place like the one Ken Kesey described in *One Flew Over the Cuckoo's Nest,* a book I read and reread a dozen times. Even though she'd never uttered my name, she was still my sister. There were moments when she would make eye contact with me now, something she never did before she went to school, and sometimes I would hear her giggle as she finished a 1000-piece jigsaw puzzle faster than any other human being. That beautiful head of cinnamon curls was brushed most days, and those Chicklet teeth were still the envy of anyone lucky enough to see her smile. I wondered, though I would never know, if Arlene burned those matches for any reason other than her love of fire. The blaze began where the baby slept; had she finally rid herself of his annoying noise-making? It was her secret to keep.

I thought about Twig, who never caught a break, who needed little more in this world than to feel loved, and never did. When Nana died of lung cancer two years after the fire, there was still a wall between the two most important women in my life, a fact that saddens me still. On another day, I would contemplate my own future. It seemed open to possibility if I was wise enough to always ask myself: "What would my mother do?" and then do the opposite.

I considered the fates of William Sparhawk and Bernard Ducharme, who stole a green Chevy Impala and wrapped it around a tree, making themselves eligible for the "In Memoriam" page of our high school yearbook. When I learned of their deaths, I was as emotionless as Arlene, and I realized then that I was capable of holding grudges. It had been six months since I'd seen Deborah Rice. Rumors of pregnancy and the story that she'd been sent to the Catholic nun's "home for whores" to hide her shame had been verified by Mrs. Hastings.

Riding home from the prison that held my uncle, I felt decades older than every kid I'd ever known.

Mostly, I thought about the irony of how I'd spent my time reading about heroes, while searching for an Atticus Finch in real life, believing that no one could ever live up to the fictionalized decency of Harper Lee's protagonist. Heroes, I had discovered, are not without flaws. Heroes have warts and quirks and addictions; they are not men or women who always do the right thing. Sometimes –

sometimes - heroes are the people who have done exactly the wrong thing, and spend their time just trying to make things right again.

About the Author

Since 1995, Janice Harvey has been the lead columnist for the independent newspaper Worcester Magazine, winning numerous awards for excellence in humor, and serious column writing and reporting, from the New England Better Newspaper Association. In 2012, Harvey published a collection of her favorite columns for local readers to enjoy. Harvey recently retired after 30 years in public education and lives in Massachusetts, surrounded by kids and grandkids, while working on a second novel set in her beloved city of Worcester.

What Other Writers Say About Janice

"Janice Harvey is a treasure. Smart, cynical, wickedly funny, and honest. She can make readers laugh, cry, and think – sometimes all at the same time. She can turn a phrase like nobody's business, and is adept at cutting to the heart of the matter, allowing the reader to see things they never noticed before. Lastly, she's a hoot."

Dianne Williamson, columnist,
Worcester Telegram & Gazette

"Janice Harvey is a shy, bashful … oops, that was the blurb for Emily Dickinson. Harv is brash and fearless and has a laugh like Woody Woodpecker. True story. She once made me laugh so hard I threw my head back and smashed it on a blackboard. She writes real funny, too with a voice as distinctively "Wista" as Tubert's or the Big Guy's. More importantly, Harv – when she writes about her old man's final days or a lifelong friendship – will break your heart because she always writes from hers. She's a wicked good writer."

Paul Della Valle, writer,
Massachusetts Troublemakers

"Janice Harvey has good eyes. And a chip on her shoulder nearly as big as the heart in her chest. When she sits down to make sense of a world of hard streets, hardboiled cops, good kids, mean girls, lifetime buddies and disgusting politicos – the world of Worcester and beyond – her wiseass side battles with the softie to see who can spin the story best. The ebb and flow of this donnybrook molds Harvey's columns into magical, essential, pictures of the real life of a real woman in the real world."

Walter Crockett,
Writer, musician

"Janice Harvey is one of Worcester's genuine voices – made unique by that unmistakable Columbus Park accent. Funny, irreverent, insightful, and engaged, Harvey has spent years recording her particular vision of the city in all its pathos, charm, and absurdity. Her column is always a delight because she understands that ole wormtown is always teeming with stories and she has the talent to capture them in clean, clear prose. Like her hometown, Harvey is gutsy, resilient, and forever cool"

Jack O'Connell,
Novelist "Box Nine"

If you have enjoyed Searching for Atticus please consider writing a review on amazon.com. Reader's reviews are very important, as they help other readers find their next book.

Made in United States
North Haven, CT
14 July 2023